APOCALYPTIC WINTER

—BOOK TWO—

An Angry Eagle Anthology

DJ Cooper
Christi Reed — S P Oldham
Albert Moss — C.A. Moll — Susan G. Isenberg
Jill Davies — D. Ryan Buford
Conny fuller — Tammy Fahey — C. J. Roberts
G. Neil Trochymchuk

https://AngryEaglePublishing.com

——

Finding many of these wonderful writers is as
easy as finding your way into the social groups on
Facebook.
Check them out
Written Apocalypse
https://Facebook.com/groups/writtenapocalypse

Sign up for the Newsletter
https://go.reachmail.net/SubscriptionForm/8a7
a5bc9-8ab4-43cb-a3db-ac27000c9523/fullpage

FORWARD

The authors were given a prompt

—

"One of the most challenging things about an apocalyptic tale is the weather. Can you describe an apocalyptic event from the perspective of winter survival? Will your characters be miserable, or will they be joyful? Is there happiness or will it only show the misery?"

The choices are up to the authors on a few conditions:

All of the following words must be included in the story

★Christmas Tree★

★Serving Spoon★

★Bear★

★Secret★

★Scarf★

CONTENTS

CHAPTER 1 — THE SHIFT

The child's screams, muffled by the blanket of fresh snow, could still be heard with regularity. An inconsolable child, even in the before; was now more so a reminder of the state of the world. Each time she was forbidden to do something or was not given her way, the child screamed as though she were being injured. Ever since the summer, we'd heard it day in and day out. This child, with fits of temper screeching at others around her, was a compass. Despite all that had gone wrong, there was something that remained normal in it all. Curious about that little girl, who is still just as inconsolable; the conversation often shifted towards wonder. Wondering if the child was now hungry, hurt, or still just inconsolable.

It's been a bit over a month since it all happened, and the Christmas Tree still stood in the corner. A reminder of the Christmas that never came. That's what the family hunkered down in the small apartment had taken to calling it. It's cold in the north and a Nor'easter... was on the horizon. More snow was coming and finding supplies was already getting precarious.

The small corner store that pretty much only carried beer had long since been emptied of everything including the racks. There was speculation about why the racks went missing, but the group that carried them off had a large truck full of strange items, and one day they'd simply added the racks too. Things sat askew in the back of the truck. Unlikely things, like the "You're in bear country" sign, an old bed frame, some cans of paint, a few hoses, rakes, lawn chairs, and even the lid of a dumpster. It was strange to see such a menagerie of items being collected when food was so desperately needed.

***

It was last month, about a week before Christmas when the lights suddenly went out. Most just assumed it was from the snowstorm, but soon realized it was much more when the power never returned. The small northeastern town was blanketed in about a foot of snow and those living there, hunkered down like they'd done time and again. They never bothered to investigate.

It was around this time that Jessie and Camron came to visit with their two children, Ashley and Keith. They'd barely removed their coats when it happened, and Ashley tripped over her scarf running to their room. Jessie, Darcy's daughter, and her family had come to spend the holiday season. Darcy loved those grandbabies and was thrilled to see them all. They'd stay two whole weeks until after the first of the year and Darcy made sure to have all of their favorite foods on hand and plenty of them. Darcy always kept a little something extra in the house just in case. Between that and the bumper crops this year they were not hungry... Yet.

She'd made out good at the farm markets and was busy throughout the fall canning up everything she could, the whole spare room was full of the goodies, many of which she'd planned to send back with the kids.

The pantry was still fairly stocked with canned vegetables, meats, and jams. There were still plenty of beans and pickles, but the pasta and rice were getting low. The flour was gone and there didn't seem to be any way they were going to get more. Darcy was becoming fearful of the gangs. They recently had been going house to house in search of supplies. Darcy lived on the third floor and vowed to never complain again. At one time it was troubling to carry the groceries up the stairs, but an inconvenience she was glad for now.

Her son lived across the hall with his wife, which made her feel safer when she'd first moved there. She still missed her small farm and was beginning to consider trying to make it there. Each tenant in the one building complex had added some supplies for building security. They had a meeting together with the others in the building to make plans and board up the lower floors, barricading the outer hallway door. They felt safe, but she knew it wouldn't last and with that Nor'easter barreling down on them she feared things might get worse.

***

No one knew what exactly happened, but things have been strange. There was a violent quake at the same time the power went out. Something strange for this area of the country, quakes were not common. Another thing they found concerning was that the clouds seemed to never clear. Darcy couldn't remember seeing the sun even once this past month, but it felt like the light would appear on the wrong side of the sky when it was clear enough to catch a glimpse of the small rounded light area that hung in the northeast section of the sky each morning.

Her son Cory came over and waved her out into the hallway. "Hey Ma, I've been noting some weird stuff."

"Me too," she said, nodding to him.

In unison, they both said, "The sun is wrong."

She peered at him with a sideways look waiting for him to say more. But he glanced in the direction of the neighboring apartment whose door had cracked open about an inch, then closed quietly when he looked over.

"I've also noticed some of the neighbors have been lurking around at night," he whispered.

"Let's go inside," she said, glancing over her shoulder.

"I didn't want to freak Jessie out," he grimaced. "You know how she gets."

"It'll be alright." She waved him inside, but before she closed the door, his wife Missy, peeked out of their apartment.

"Everything ok?" She asked.

"Yes," Darcy replied. "C'mon over, let's get to fixing dinner and have a family meeting."

"I'll come round," Missy said and nodded, closing the door.

They shared a balcony and Missy deadbolted their door and went around to the other apartment from the balcony.

"Babe," she said, kissing Cory. We need to stay on the shoveling, the path on the balcony is starting to get deep again."

Cameron hopped up, "I got this, I need a little fresh air anyway."

Darcy waved Cory into the kitchen. Her son stood a full foot taller than her and he had to duck going through the entry. Jessie and Missy joined them. Cory slumped as if they'd just rained on his parade. He widened his eyes at his mother and tilted his head toward the other room.

"Aww geez Cory, just spit it out. Whatever it is, will be without a doubt something terrible and as usual, you're probably right too," Jessie blurted out rolling her eyes.

"Listen, Jess, it's just speculation."

"So?" She stood, hands on her hips waiting for him to say something.

"So… What?" He bugged his eyes at her as though they were still kids and getting ready to stick their tongues out behind Darcy's back.

"Go ahead Cory, she'll have to hear it sooner or later," Darcy said. "And don't you roll your eyes at him either little miss," she flashed a look and scolded Jessie, waving the serving spoon at her.

Missy giggled at her and winked.

"Ma and I have both noticed that the sun is in the wrong place in the sky."

"Yea, I saw that. No amazing secret there, big brother," Jessie said shrugging and stuffing another chunk of the canned peaches she was spooning up for the kids in her mouth.

"Well, what that means," Cory glared at her. "Is that nothing is going to get right, the power is not coming back, and we are both just about out of propane."

"Okay," she shrugged. "What are we supposed to do about it."

"There is a nor'easter building. Right ma?" Cory looked expectantly at Darcy.

"That's what my bones are telling me," she croaked and rubbed at her elbow.

"Oh, good grief, you two are nuts," Jessie said, grabbing the two bowls and marching out of the kitchen. She barged back into the kitchen and looked at them wide-eyed. "What hell are we gonna do?" The tears welling up in her eyes as she glanced toward the children.

"We have to go to the farm... Tonight," he said.

"Tonight?" Jessie asked.

"Yea, we gotta beat the storm, and besides, it is not safe here anymore. I think these neighbors are running out of food and propane. I checked the tanks for some of them yesterday when I was outside, and they are empty. If they know we have food and heat they are gonna come for it."

"How are we supposed to get there?" Jessie practically yelled.

"Shhhhh..." Missy cooed at her.

"Missy and I have the two snow machines; we can pull the sleds the kids brought plus the skiff round back. It is big and will hold most of the supplies."

Darcy was nodding, but not saying anything. It was only nine miles but in the snow that is a long way.

"We also have the canoe," Missy said expectantly.

Cody winced, "I don't think that will work, the

6

bottom isn't flat."

"But, is the house ok?" Jessie asked.

Darcy nodded but before she could speak Cameron interrupted. "Someone is at the door." His face white, "they don't look friendly, peeking at them through the peephole."

Cody looked out, "It's Joe from the first floor. I'll go round," he said and headed for the porch.

A few moments later they could hear the door open and Cody speaking. Darcy put her eye up to the peephole and watched, while Cameron stood at the ready holding the shotgun.

They could hear the muffled voices, "Hey man, what's up," Cody asked the man.

"Listen, we know you have some food." The man shoved Cody. Darcy's grip on the knob tightened.

"Woah, Woah, Woah," Cody said. "What do you mean coming up here and shoving me around."

"We ran out of food days ago, it ain't fair you still got some," Joe retorted.

"Scuse me?" Cody said, standing a little taller. If that was possible, he was already six foot five.

"We had that meeting, and everyone agreed we would work together."

"To secure the building. I ain't gotta feed you too," Cody crossed his arms. "Besides, we do have a few cans of beans and fruit, but that's all. If I give it to you? What are we supposed to eat?"

The man shrank and Darcy's grip on the doorknob relaxed slightly. His head hung and he turned to leave.

"C'mon, now wait a minute, Joe. How is Alice?" Cody coaxed him.

"She's been sick with a bad cold," the man said

dejectedly. "I don't know what to do about it."

Cody patted him on the back and said, "Wait right here."

He left the door wide open and made a show of opening and closing all the cabinets. Then went to the bathroom. "C'mon in Joe," he called out.

The man hesitantly stepped through the door. Worry clouded his eyes and a tremor shook him. He wanted the food but knew he was no match for Cody. He was scared and Cody knew it.

"Ok," he said, rearranging some things on the table. "There are two cans of beans, corn, some bouillon, a can of mixed fruit, and half a box of cheerios."

The man looked up at him, surprise covered his face.

Cody handed him a bottle of Nyquil, "This is the best I can do, we don't even have this much."

The man held the can of beans and looked up at him. "But..."

"I was thinking about trying to hunt tomorrow, a lousy can of beans and some cereal isn't gonna make that big of a difference. Let's hope for a big buck," Cody said, slapping his hand on the man's back.

Just as Joe got to the doorway, Cody's hand clamped down on his shoulder. "I meant to ask you... Why were you beating on the other door?"

Joe hung his head. "Because she's an old lady and I figured... Well, Ummm."

Cody released the man's shoulder and he began to scurry down the stairwell. At the first landing, Cody called out, "Oh, Joe?"

Joe paused, looking up at him. "Don't ever try to bully my mom again. If I don't kill you... she will." He smiled and closed the door.

The man hurried through the halls back to his apartment and slammed the door, a loud CLICK locking the deadbolt.

Cody went back around from the porch and found the others already packing up the food, blankets, and warm clothing.

Darcy and Cody plotted their path to the farm. It was nine miles but taking the trails if they weren't too soft would save them a couple of miles.

"Mom and Missy will drive the snow machines, the kids will ride with one, and Jessie you will ride with the other," he said looking at his sister. "Everyone will wear or wrap up in the blankets, it will help keep warm but also leave space for other stuff in the boat."

"Didn't you see a bear in those woods?" Missy asked.

"Don't worry, they should be hibernating," Cody assured her.

He looked around the room at the wide eyes, they were all scared of the cold and what was out there.

The small group of family members quietly carried their things to the boat down the back stairwell off the porch. They'd start the snow machines at the last possible moment and be gone. Cameron and Cody jogged beside each of them pushing when they got bogged down. They were about a mile down the trail when they heard gunshots and stopped. Behind them rose a bright yellow light in the distance. Their building was the next one raided by the gangs and they'd set it ablaze. They could hear the screams of their neighbors. Darcy turned back to the trail and hit the lever for the gas, lurching the machine forward.

About DJ Cooper

DJ Cooper is a prominent author of the apocalypse with the Dystopia series and other short works. Currently, a student at Southern New Hampshire University to advance her bachelor's degree she now studies for her Master of Fine Arts Degree in Marketing.

She also writes informative articles for magazines such as The Odyssey, Prepper Survival guide, and Prepare Magazine. Her books are post-apocalyptic fiction, focusing on real life scenarios and offering prepper information both within its pages and as a resource.

She currently lives in New England but worked in and around the Cincinnati, Ohio area flipping houses. During that time, she spent much of it in the areas of Kentucky she writes about in the Dystopia books, offering a firsthand view into her locations.

It's been more than a couple of years that she's been known as an internet radio host and the executive producer of the Prepper Podcast Radio Network KPRN-DB, you can hear archived shows at http://www.prepperpodcast.com. Find her and others in the author group. https://www.facebook.com/groups/writtenapocalypse/

Follow her and find her books

https://authoroftheapocalypse.com

https://www.facebook.com/AuthorDJCooper/

https://www.goodreads.com/author/show/6430420.D_J_Cooper

CHAPTER 2 — TEN THINGS

Camilla, "Cammi" as her mother and father always called her, clutched her mother's diary to her chest as if she could absorb the love written on these precious pages. Tears of loneliness and grief filled her eyes to overflowing. They sat perched on her lashes momentarily, seeming to defy gravity until the weight of them begged for release. They glistened in the early morning light like diamonds as they traveled over her smooth tanned skin.

Angrily, Cammi swiped the tears from her face with the back of her hand, flopped down hard onto her mother's bed, and opened the diary to the last entry her mother wrote.

December 25th, 2020
My dearest Cammi, you are the love of my life and my heart. Isn't life a bitch? LOL! I know I am fading... you know I am fading. There are things I have.... I have to tell you before time runs out. Sorry

sweets, another coughing fit, they are more regular and persistent now. This virus that plagues the world has changed our lives forever. In my dreams I am giving you away at your wedding. In my dreams I am holding your children, my grandchildren, in my arms. I know deep within my soul one day you will be a fabulous mother. BUT, you must survive what is coming; I have seen it in my dreams.

I lay here listening to machines humming and alarming when someone's oxygen level drops. And as I watch, the nurses scramble into disposable gowns, gloves, and face shields in a vain attempt to help. I hear the sounds of other patients hacking up their lungs, desperately gasping trying to draw in enough air. I wonder how long it will be before I am that way.

I so wish they would let you come and see me, but they say it is unsafe and for the best that you do not. I would never forgive myself if my love for you caused you to go through this.

If you are reading this, it means I am gone. So, listen up kiddo… what I have to say is important. It very well may save your life.

First you have to be strong. You have to control your fear. When you let fear control you, you will make bad decisions… and you cannot afford to do that. NOT NOW!

#1. In the Christmas tree box, in the attic, you will find a metal box. I want you go get it. Inside, you will find plans and maps for an emergency route and a location where you should go. If what I think is going to happen, does indeed happen, you are going to need it.

#2. Take my credit cards from the box and buy

as much food as you can. Stuff that will be okay to store long term, and only needs hot water to prepare. I have cash stashed inside the throw pillows on my bed.... You know, the ones you always complained were lumpy. LOL! Save the cash for when the ATM's stop working, which they eventually will.

#3. Your world is about to change drastically, sweetheart. Watch the news carefully, keep informed. Read between the lines and do not believe everything you hear or see. Trust no-one! Follow your gut.

#4. While you have running water, electricity, and gas, cook the foods that will spoil first and collect as much water as you can. Fill the bathtubs, pots, pans, jugs; whatever you can get your hands on. Do no open the bottled water YET. Save it for when the water stops flowing. Also, remember, there is water in the hot water heater. You can save rain water in the trash cans after you clean them with bleach, use this water to flush the toilet, until the sewage starts to back up in the lines. And if you filter it through several layers of fabric you can use it to bathe and wash your clothes if you have to.

#5. In the basement, at the back wall under the stairs, remove the baseboard... it is fastened with Velcro. There you will find an AR-15 wrapped in oil cloth, a scope and ammo. I know I kept it secret from you. Sorry, love. It was better that way. Why do you think we took all those training classes with Jeff Motes? Not just because they were fun. They were, but I wanted you to be prepared, just in case. Clean it and load it, have it close at all times.

#6. In my closet, underneath the shoe rack, the floor tiles are not glued down... they just look like they are. Under them is a hollow space with a cheap, hideously green scarf, which is wrapped around several rolls of old silver dimes, nickels, and quarters. These you will need if the banks close and you need to barter for supplies later down the road.

#7. Now... go to the family room. The picture on the mantle of your dad, when he killed that bear... lean it forward and the bottom of the mantle will open. No, you did not break it; it is supposed to do that. Your father's 1911 pistol is in there. It's yours now. Load it and keep it on your person at all times. YOU CAN DO THIS!

#8. In the kitchen, behind that old tarnished serving spoon that's hanging on the wall... you know, the one we found while out antique hunting that one day. There are keys taped to its back. They unlock the guest house basement and cabinet doors. I think you will be surprised at what you find there.

#9. Go to the garage and pack the backpacks, one at a time, with full water bottles. I know this sounds weird... but trust me. I want you to wear one every day, all day, everywhere you go. Walk in it, run in it, and climb in it. You know how heavy they get on long walks, which is what I am afraid you will be doing.... SOON. Remember, water is heavy. If you can't carry it all day, every day... then, you are carrying too much, and you need to lighten your load. I hope you have enough time to do this. It is important to build your strength and stamina. START NOW...! DO NOT WAIT...! I REPEAT, DO NOT WAIT!

#10. In the library, on the 5th shelf from the bottom, in the center you will see books titled: *Living Ready Pocket First Aid; Alton's Antibiotics and Infectious*

Disease; and *The Pocket Guide to Prepper Knots.* Put these with your supplies. Also, if you have room and the strength, take my tablet and the solar charger. There are a ton of books stored on it which will teach you and keep you company. Don't forget the ear buds, sweet. These are the basics I want you to carry. I know, you are wondering why only three books. Well, books, like water, are heavy. They will also take up valuable room in your pack. Remember, think excess weight. Carry as many multipurpose items as possible. I know you have heard the phrase, "One is none, Two is one," but redundancy sometimes is your enemy.

Promise me you will do these 10 things first. You will have to shed your grief and mourn later. The papers in that metal box in #1 will guide you further. Good luck, My Love.

My love will travel with you every step of the way.

MOM

*****

Cammi flung herself back against the mattress and wrapped her arms around her body, squeezing as tight as her young arms would allow. At seventeen, she was now an orphan. Her father had died two years ago from cancer and now her mother was gone. Seven days, just seven days before her 18th birthday. The world was turning to shit. She gave in to the grief, allowing her misery to pour out in throat-wrenching sobs that convulsed her body. For this moment in time… she was a child in despair, alone, lonely, and frightened. All she had were these words her mother had written out of love. Words meant to save her life.

****

Hours later Cammi rose from her bed, snuffling as children do, and peered in the mirror attached to her dresser. Her inner sadness stared back. Her eyelids were swollen; the whites of her eyes were bloodshot and still burned from her tears, and a nose red enough to guide Santa's sleigh topped off the face which gazed despondently back at her.

Cammi went into her bathroom, splashed cold water on her face, patted it dry and brushed away the nasty, sticky film coating her tongue and teeth. She returned to her bedroom and picked up her mother's diary and reread her last entry. She read down the list and stopped at #4. Collect as much water as you can. She placed the stopper in the tub and sink, turned the cold water tap on full blast, then walked to her mother's bathroom and did the same. After both tubs were filled to the rim she continued reading. She walked to the hall and grasped the pull cord of the attic ladder and pulled the hatch down, unfolded the ladder, and ascended into the place where memories were stored.

SCAVENGER HUNT
#1.

As she climbed the ladder to the attic, she wondered what had her mother been up to. So many secrets, and why hide stuff all over the place? Bright light flickered to life when she flipped the switch on the wall next to the opening in the floor. The side walls were lined with neatly stacked cardboard boxes, from floor to ceiling. Cammi read the labels as she walked past them until she found the Christmas tree box, nestled at the end of the far wall. Thousands of memories she would never relive floated across her heart as she pulled it from atop the stack. She stilled herself before lifting the lid.

At first glance all she saw was the artificial limbs and tips of the imitation fir tree. They'd had so much fun decorating it each year. When she removed the top section of the tree, the metal box sat within the prickly stems. The garish red and green paint which covered the box seemed out of place in the otherwise orderly room. She reached in grasping the handle and was surprised at its weight.

"I found it, Mama," she whispered, pulling the cool metal to her chest.

She closed the lid of the box, turned off the light, and descended the ladder, with one last look around before folding the ladder back on itself. The hinges squealed in protest as she let the pull rope slide through her fingers until the door softly thudded closed.

Cammi sat the box on the dining room table, slid the latch release, and raised the lid. Inside lay a manila envelope with her name scrolled across the front, written in her mother's handwriting. Inside there were several maps of the area focusing on Vulcan Park and Red Mountain Park. One map was an enlarged street map with marks highlighting: restaurants, drug stores, sporting goods stores, and grocery stores... along with a list of apartment complexes and neighborhoods to avoid. The Birmingham Botanical Gardens was highlighted as a source of fresh water. A photo of the Vulcan statue which stands 56 feet above Red Mountain was included, as this would be the highest point to observe the city from a distance.

Vulcan Park was only one mile from Cammi's home, with plenty of wooded areas to travel through if needed. There were also two other photos, one of the Trail Map of Red Mountain Park and the other a photo of what looked like a cement block bunker. Cammi read the notes scribbled along the margins and recognized the structure as Old No. 11 coal ore mine's entrance that had just been opened recently for visitors. She studied the maps closer and realized her mother had mapped a route through the park. It covered the paths she would need to take over walking and hiking trails, and across swinging bridges, showing her destination. It was a seven-mile hike to Old No. 11. Since the mine was only listed on the park's Trail Map, her mother had traced several routes leading to the mine in hopes that Cammi would have a safe place to hide.

Cammi shook the envelope over the table and a slip of paper floated out. "Study these maps, memorize them. You know shug... just in case." It was signed X's and O's. "P.S. Cammi, if you lose communications, TV, phone, internet... climb the Vulcan. And if you see fires or hear gunfire.... Run, Cammi.... Run!"

Cammi tucked the paper in her jean pocket. While she was in the kitchen she found and filled every pot, pitcher, pan, and jug with water from the faucet. With that task completed she found four gallons of bleach and sat them on the kitchen floor.

****

Cammi's stomach growled deep in her belly, a long gurgling sound, reminding her she hadn't eaten since getting out of bed this morning and it was not almost 2:00 p.m. in the afternoon. She opened the refrigerator and surveyed her choices. "Pizza, lasagna, peanut butter, eggs, cheese, bread, milk... and way in the back... chocolate cheesecake, apples, carrots, and oranges." Cammi removed the cheesecake. In the freezer she found, chocolate chip ice cream, chicken nuggets, deli meats, butter, broccoli, Brussels sprouts, chopped onions, diced red and green peppers, blue and black berries, mango chunks, pineapple, strawberries, and a half-full bottle of vodka. With her dessert choice made she heated the pizza in the microwave and poured a Coke over some ice. She turned on the television hoping she wouldn't hear or see bad news, which would mean she was running out of time... to run.

#1. Complete.

#2. Complete, except buying food and cash.

#3. Understood.

#4. Drinking water, collected. Bleach located. Still need to clean the trash cans and eat from the refrigerator and freezer.

Note: Wash clothes while I can use the washing machine and dryer.

#5. Basement, get AR, clean and load it, keep it close.

****

In the basement Cammi pulled the baseboard from the wall behind the stairs and removed the rifle, scope, and ammo. She removed it from the oil cloth; pulling back the charging handle to verify that is was unloaded and carried the items to the kitchen. She sat on the floor and wiped it down to remove the excess oil, disassembled it, reassembled it, attached the scope, and inserted a full magazine, chambered a round and placed it on safe.

#5. Complete.

****

#6. In Mom's closet, get the silver from the scarf from under the shoe rack.

Cammi stood in the doorway of her mother's closet looking at the mountain of shoes on the shoe rack and sighed. "This is going to be fun," she mumbled and began emptying the shoe rack. She tossed the shoes in a pile in a corner next to the door. When empty, she tugged on the heavy rack and to her surprise it slid with ease. On her hands and knees, she picked at the seams in the tile without result. "You are supposed to come up," she huffed. She removed the knife clipped inside her waistband, flipped out the blade and dug at the seams until she found a loose one and prized it out of place. Sure enough, stuffed in a hollow of the floor joists and sub-floor was that ugly green scarf. She lifted the scarf out and went back downstairs to the kitchen. She untied the scarf and counted the rolls of coins her mother had hidden which totaled one-hundred dollars.

#6. Complete.

****

#7. Family room, picture of dad on the mantle, 9mm 1911. Load it and keep it on me.

Cammi left the kitchen and walked into the family room, stood in front of the picture of her dad, grinning from ear to ear while trying to hold the black bear's head for the photo. She remembered how proud he had been. She reached for the picture frame and pulled it toward her. It didn't slide but leaned forward. She heard a click, the bottom slowly opened and there sure enough was dad's favorite pistol, a box of ammo and a holster. Remembering, she ejected the loaded magazine and racked the slide ejecting the round from the chamber. She picked the round up off the floor and re-loaded it in the magazine, inserted the magazine, chambered a round, and put it on safe before sliding it into the holster resting on her right side.

#7. Complete. "I CAN DO THIS... I CAN DO THIS... I CAN DO THIS...," she chanted as she walked back to the kitchen.

****

#8. Note: "Do this tomorrow when it is not so close to dark." Cammi was tired and unsure about going into the basement this late in the evening by herself. #9. Backpacks filled with water. Cammi was too exhausted mentally and physically and decided to tackle the water bottle filled backpacks the next morning.

****

#10. Library, books, 5th shelf-center, mom's tablet, solar charger, and ear buds. Put on table, goes in backpack.

Cammi passed through the family room into the adjoining library and stood looking at the floor to ceiling bookcase. She mentally counted 1, 2, 3, 4, 5. Just as her mom said, the books were exactly in the middle. Beside her mother's favorite reading chair on a small table laid her tablet. Cammi followed the small black wire attached to the tablet to a nearby window where the solar charger sat facing the setting sun. Cammi added the tablet and charger to the stack of books she carried. On her way out of library she brushed her fingers over the worn leather of the chair and smiled. How many times had she seen her mother quietly reading there, long into the night?

#10. Complete.

Cammi sat at the dining table with her growing pile of supplies and yawned. The sun had dipped below the horizon and an empty, hollow, quietness vibrated through the room.

****

Cammi bolted awake in a panic. The sounds of sirens and a reporter narrating a live video from the Birminham-Shuttlesworth International Airport screamed from the television. She slid from the sofa and crawled to sit in front of the screen. "Just in case," echoed in her mind.

How had mom known?

The video was a live broadcast from a news agency helicopter. What she was witnessing terrified her. The screen showed the main terminal and the Alabama Air National Guard at Sumpter Smith Air National Guard Base and five KC-135 Stratotanker refueling aircraft on the tarmac blazing. Giant orange and bright yellow fireballs roiled above the destroyed structures and decimated planes. The inferno roared and rolled, spewing oily black smoke and char into the air. The air was filled with the fumes just as the jet fuel from the refueling station exploded. Emergency crews from Army and Air Force security, Fire Response and ambulances surrounded the scene. Firefighters from Firehouse #5 which sat west of the Air Base scrambled to contain the fire.

According to the reporter several explosions

had erupted throughout the city as well... targeting all airports in and around the city, large and small, within a 120-mile swath from east to west and southward. This had effectively cut Birmingham's air capabilities off since there were no airports northward within a couple hours driving time.

Then there was silence.... The screen went black.... A message: "Complete loss of signal," was displayed across the screen.

"What the?!" Cammi questioned,

"It's not raining. Don't panic. Don't panic," she heard her mother's voice say. Remember #8, Remember the Vulcan.

****

Cammi scrambled to her feet, practically running to the table, shoving supplies aside in her haste. "Where is it?" she cried out loud. She whirled around franticly until she spied the diary lying next to the sofa where she had slept last night. Turning to the last page she reread #8. Key behind spoon on the wall, guest house basement....

"Vulcan, climb the Vulcan."

Cammi snatched the spoon from the wall, turning it over in one swift motion, removed the keys and headed toward the back door, stopped, went back to the sofa, picked up the AR-15 and slung it across her shoulder. It dangled from the 3-point sling at her knee. She touched the holster at her waist reassuring herself the 1911 was still in place, before heading out the backdoor.

****

Cammi flipped the light switch on in the basement of the guest house and her mouth formed an

"O" in astonishment. The room was filled, floor to ceiling with boxes, all labeled: Freeze Dried Meals, Medical Supplies, Personal Hygiene, Batteries, Clothes, Bedding, Camping Gear, Lighting, Water Purification, Heat, and one small box labeled, HALLOWEEN. There were cases and cases of bottled water stacked along the back wall on a pallet. Dozens of boxes of canning jars, lids, and rings sat neatly stacked beside the water, canners and propane cylinders, portable stoves, and solar panels. Cammi braced herself against the doorframe in awe.

A metal steel cabinet sat in the back-left corner, padlocked. Cammi pushed the second key into the lock and it turned effortlessly with a soft 'click' and the lock dropped open. The door opened silently, and inside, stacks of boxes of AR-15 rounds, 9mm rounds, along with a wicked looking AR-style 12-gauge semi-automatic shotgun and shells ranging from buck shot to slugs. Several stacks of spare magazines sat at the ready. "OMG!!" Cammin uttered.

Cammi opened one of the Freeze-Dried boxes and rummaged through the contents, choosing several pouches with chemical heaters, a spork, and closed the lid. From the other boxes she found a head lamp, small pocket flashlight, batteries, a small first-aid kit, a lightweight sleeping mat, waterproof matches, a Life Straw water filter, an emergency poncho, toilet paper, and wipes. Cammi eyed the HALLOWEEN box curiously, lifted the lid, and to her surprise... Smoke Bombs... all kinds. She giggled and stuffed a few in her pocket.

Cammi locked the steel cabinet, collected her supplies, turned off the lights and locked the basement door. Upstairs she checked all the windows and left, locking the door behind her before going back to the main house.

#8. Complete.

****

After adding the new supplies to the pile on the table she went into the garage and picked out one of the light brown backpacks. She placed it in a chair and packed the new supplies along with the first aid book and a couple bottles of water. An extra magazine for the 1911 went into her front left pocket and another in her back left pocket of her jeans. She clipped a folding knife onto her waistband, clipped the house keys to a lanyard around her neck and studied the maps. The diary went into the main compartment of the pack, resting on the other supplies.

The Vulcan statue was one mile from Cammi's house on 21st Avenue S and was in a heavily wooded park land. She prayed the elevator in the visitor center was still working. If not, she had a lot of steps to climb to the observation deck... over one-thousand feet above the ground. Since the statue faced east, she would be able to have a clear view of the city, with the international airport due north and east. She double-checked the doors and windows making sure they were locked, turned off all the lights and locked the door. Cammi eased around the west side of the house, into the cover of trees between her house and Sahara Direct Security System's building which faced Richard Arlington Jr. Rd. There, she would have enough cover to monitor the traffic and her surroundings. She looked at her watch, 11:00 a.m., "Damn, almost lunch hour traffic." Once she crossed Richard Arlington Jr. Rd., she could follow the parks tree line around the parking lot to the statue lawn. The park closed at 10:00 p.m., this would give her plenty of time to wait until all or most of the visitors left, if there were any.

Cammi sucked in a deep breath, stilled herself and sprinted from the trees to the back of the building. There were no cars parked at the back, which was odd, she let out her breath when she saw the security camera pointing at her, "Shit." Her heart pounded in her ears and she began to sweat as she waited and wondered if anyone would pop out the back entrance to investigate. No one came, after five minutes the streets were silent.

Cammi peered around the corner of the building. Nothing. No cars, no trucks, nothing driving down Richard Arlington. This was really strange; there should be vehicle traffic. She held the AR close to her body as she crouched low against the wall trying to become smaller. Deep breaths in through the nose... slow breaths out through the mouth... while she prayed her knees wouldn't buckle. Time slowed as she sprinted across the five-laned road into the tree-line. Cammi hooked her right arm around a tree before stumbling onto the park's entrance road. She squatted and watched. Still no cars, no people that she could see. She flitted from tree to tree until she was directly across from the visitor's entrance. She synched the AR in tight to her body and ran full-out across to the opening between the statue and the elevator tower, there she paused to catch her breath, pushed the up button, and listened.... She could hear whirring and then... 'ding,' the elevator door slid open. Cammi stepped inside to the back corner, leaned over, and braced her hands on her knees as she tried to control the urge to vomit. The adrenaline was taking control, her mouth was dry, and her body shook with fatigue. Breathing heavily, she watched the bottom of the door. When it slid open, she stepped out onto the steel grate walkway into the open air. The breeze cooled her sweat and lessened her nausea.

The view of her hometown brought tears to her eyes. To her north she could see the billowing towers of black smoke rising from the International airport several miles away. Numerous smoke towers rose above the cityscape, within the seven miles to the airport and beyond. Dotted all around the city small fires burned and gray smoke rose and mingled with the clouds. The distant sound of fireworks popping could be heard then sirens blared and then more popping, Gunfire, her brain screamed... "NO, what has happened?"

Cammi leaned against the Vulcans' tower and slid to the grate. She pulled a water bottle from her pack, took a long drink, watched, and listened. As the sun lowered in the east, the shadows stretched, and the sounds from the streets increased. What once sounded faraway was coming closer. The sounds of gunfire were distinct now and she could tell the difference between rifle and handgun, the constant whine and scream of ambulances, police, and fire engines, were discernable. Sometimes a loud boom would echo off the mountain and the tower would vibrate beneath her. As the sun crept lower to the horizon, through the smoke and smog fires flickered, spreading like spider webs in the distance. Cammi stood adjusted her rifle high and ready, slipped her backpack over her shoulders and turned her back on this new world. A world she did not want to face but had no choice but to do so. Home, she had to get home and follow the plan, now!

****

Derek lowered the binoculars when the girl he had followed stepped into the elevator at the statue. He watched her stand at the railing, watching the city burn. He watched her slide to the grate. He watched the sadness and horror cross her face. Why had she stayed there so long? He melted into the shadows of the park as she emerged from the elevator and sprinted across the open spaces into the trees. He followed her through the darkness, almost losing her from time to time. "Damn" she was fast and quiet. He noted her confidence with the weapons she carried, which only came from experience and training. Who was this slip of a girl and why was she here alone?

****

Cammi sprinted through the trees toward Richard Arlington Road and paused when a branch behind her snapped. She turned her ear to the side and listened, took a few steps further and stopped again. A chill ran across her arms and the hairs rose on the nape of her neck. She quickly scanned both directions of the now empty street and dashed across in a full run until she reached the back corner of the Sahara Direct Security Systems building and slid to a stop when she rounded the corner. She stood ready, listening. There, she heard them. Fast footsteps on the paved lot. Closer… closer… slower now…. She squatted low to the ground and waited.

When Derek heard the girl run across the road,

he picked up his pace to a fast jog and stopped at the road. He couldn't hear her footsteps any longer. "Dammit, where did she go?" He wondered. After crossing the road, he slowed his pace to a cautious walk, intent on listening for her. There was total silence. He wasn't familiar with this area but knew the building sat next to a neighborhood with plenty of trees she could be hiding in. With, arrogance and pride in his abilities he continued toward the back-parking lot. As soon as he passed the back of the building a firm voice spoke out of the darkness and a blinding light pulsed in his face, blinding him. He froze.

When the stranger stepped past the building Cammi called to him, "What do you want?!" she demanded, aiming the flashlight's LED light at his head.

Derek broke out in a belly laugh and when he was able to speak said, "Damn little girl, you are good. You totally got me."

About the Author — Susan G. Isenberg

Susan is the mother or two, grandmother of three. She's a semi-retired nurse and has always had a preparedness mindset and a problem solver by nature. Hunting, fishing, gardening and food preservation are a way of life, not a hobby.

She shares from experience what it is like to be hungry and scared for your life.

She is a survivor.

CHAPTER 3 — ANGIE'S DILEMMA

It was a dark and stormy night, as the large white snowflakes fell on the discarded Christmas tree. Angie struggled to believe that it had been less than a month before when the tree was decorating someone's house. She thought of the colorfully decorated tree, with lots of presents under it, highlighting someone's living room. Now, it laid crumpled on its side in a dirty snowdrift. Still, she supposed that the tree had suffered less in the apocalypse than had the house which had once held it.

As she trudged through the deepening snow and struggled to push the salvaged grocery store shopping cart, she tightened the scarf around her head. She reflected on her own situation. The war had come quickly, with no one expecting that a minor international trade dispute would result in global thermonuclear war. When the nuclear warheads had detonated high overhead, not only had they destroyed the electrical power grid and anything electronic with a massive EMP wave, but the arcs they caused had resulted in a majority of the homes catching fire and burning to the ground. Panicked people, in thousands of cities, had struggled to call the fire departments on telephones which no longer worked. Angie's apartment was one of those destroyed in the fires. She escaped while only carrying a stuffed teddy bear and wearing the clothes on her back.

She continually asked herself why she had grabbed that small stuffed bear as she was running out of the flaming building. After all, it seemed silly for a 23-year-old woman to be carrying a stuffed bear with her. But maybe it was because the bear had been a present from her deceased father all those years ago. Or, maybe it was because it reminded her of happier times. Or, maybe her mind had shattered when the bombs exploded. Or, maybe it was because it was all she could find in the darkness and smokiness of her burning apartment. Whatever the reason, she vowed to protect Teddy in the uncertain times she found herself in.

As a feral dog howled in the distance, Angie pushed the shopping cart a bit faster through the deepening drifts. The cold metal of the handle stung her bare fingers, as her feet sloshed through puddles of partially melted snow, soaking through the black tennis shoes she wore. Still, she pushed on through the darkness of night, until she reached the fire-damaged brick farmhouse on the back of an overgrown farm.

She quickly stashed the shopping cart behind the derelict house, as she looked around for any sign of someone watching her. Having seen no one, she rapidly tipped a flowerpot over and retrieved the key to the concrete-block toolshed from its secret hiding spot. She walked along a set of pitted and broken gray concrete steppingstones, to reach the weathered wooden door of the toolshed. After quickly knocking twice in rapid succession, she inserted the key into the lock and opened the door. Once inside, she pushed the door shut and turned the lock, to secure herself inside of the small building.

Angie tossed a few more scraps of wood into the large cast iron pot which she was using as a makeshift stove. As the twigs and sticks ignited, they provided the only illumination inside of the tiny, windowless building. She was relieved to find her younger stepsister, Lisa, laying comfortably on a cot in the corner of the frigid building, covered by a number of soot-stained blankets. With a gleam in her eye, Angie held up the results of her evening's scavenging trip, two cans of Lima beans. Quickly, she grabbed a silvery metal bowl and a bent serving spoon from her meager supply of kitchen items, which she had salvaged from a burned house. She then pulled out a can opener and opened the two cans, which she dumped into the bowl. Angie carried the bowl over to Lisa, who sat up in the makeshift bed. The two took turns eating the beans with the single serving spoon.

After the simple meal, Angie removed the blue jacket and the green blouse she had been wearing, both of which were soaked with water from melting snow and hung them up to dry. She then toweled herself off, using a scavenged, filthy orange towel, which she then hung next to the jacket and blouse. Thankful for the walls of the shed acting as a windbreak, she climbed onto the cot with Lisa and snuggled close to her, as she positioned her teddy bear between them. It was only a few moments after she pulled the stack of blankets over them both that she was asleep.

Angie wasn't sure what time it was when she awoke. Time had ceased to have any real meaning for her, other than the difference between daytime and darkness. During the daytime, she preferred to stay in the shed, in order to avoid being noticed by the other scavengers. The only safe time for her to leave the shed was in the darkness, when she could carefully scour the burned buildings in the nearby town, for any sort of food or useful tool. She had discovered many twisted and melted pieces of metal and many exploded cans, but useful items were few and far between.

There were many things Angie needed, with the primary one being food. No longer could she make a quick trip to the corner market to buy food. Instead, she was reduced to scavenging for it in the partially burned and abandoned buildings of the town. And, she was in competition with the other survivors. Even worse, was the fact that many of the other survivors could be brutally violent. She had been forced several times to drop the cans of food, which she had scavenged, in order to make a quick escape from another survivor who was intent on taking her food... or worse.

Angie wasn't worried about the other survivors just taking her food. She knew that many of the men would take something much more valuable from her. And, while she was a firm believer in the commandment, *"Thou shall not murder,"* she realized that it wouldn't be murder if she were defending herself. Still, the lack of a weapon made any defense she could offer quite limited.

Of course, Angie wasn't only worried about her safety. The safety of her younger stepsister was also on her mind. While, with the appropriate clothing, she could pass herself off as a chubby man, there was no chance of camouflaging her younger sister, Lisa, with her blonde hair and feminine build, definitely appeared female. Thus, Angie insisted that Lisa remain inside the toolshed, while she did all of the scavenging.

Lisa, however, being a teenager, lusted after the excitement of scavenging. She constantly begged Angie to include her on some of the trips. Not only did she desire the excitement, but she also wanted to help Angie supply themselves with food and other items they so desperately needed. However, Angie would not relent on insisting that Lisa stay in the safety of the shed.

Angie climbed out from under the pile of blankets and made her way to where her blouse and jacket were hanging. She quickly slipped them both on, which did little to alleviate the penetrating cold which had soaked the toolshed. She added the last of the wood scraps to the cast iron pot and blew on them, until a tiny flame erupted from the base of the pot. She held her chilled hands over the tiny flame, desperate to soak up any of the heat that she could.

Once her hands were warmed, Angie stood up and walked to the door. She carefully lifted the piece of heavy cardboard she had taped over the tiny window in the top of the door and peered out into the dim light of a sunset. She sighed heavily as she realized that it was almost time for her to go on another scavenging run, but that she'd have to do it through the heavy snow which had accumulated during the day.

Reluctantly, she walked over to the cot and retrieved her precious teddy bear, which she secured in one of the pockets of her jacket. She then grabbed a small pry-bar, which she had found on one of her scavenging trips and tucked it in her belt. Finally, she leaned down and kissed Lisa's head, before she turned and made her way out of the toolshed. She locked the door and concealed the key in the secret hiding place before she headed toward the town.

Angie tried to take a different path to the town every night so that someone couldn't set an ambush for her. The previous night, she had traveled along the narrow country road, which wound itself between the small farms. But tonight, she had decided to travel along the bank of the small, frozen creek, which crossed the back of the farm. She cursed mildly as she realized that she was leaving a very visible trail in the heavy snow. So, she walked for a quarter of an hour in the opposite direction before she reversed her course and headed back to the town.

After an hour of hiking through the deep snow, Angie finally made it to the outskirts of the town. The smell of smoke still lingered in the air, with most coming from the remains of so many burned houses. However, a small portion came from campfires built by other survivors. Angie was very suspicious of the other survivors, given that many of them had become violent once the rule of law had disappeared. She carefully skirted the campfires and restricted her scavenging to the demolished buildings far away from other survivors.

Angie had realized, long ago, that there was little food nor tools to be found in the burned buildings. However, detached sheds and garages often contained usable tools. And, stalled cars sometimes had food stashed in them by people returning from the grocery. Given that she had forsaken the shopping cart and that she could only carry a limited amount of material, she intentionally limited her scavenging to food, which was more valuable to her than tools were.

She darted from shed to garage to abandoned car, in the darkness and shadows of the night. Her greatest fear, besides running into another survivor who would prove to be violent, was running into a feral dog. Many of the dogs which had been pets were no longer cared for and had become feral, hunting anything they could for food. And, Angie realized, that included humans, as well as other former pets. She realized that the world had become a very violent place, literally a dog-eat-dog world.

A white Toyota Camry, with the trunk open, was parked in front of an ash-pile in the shape of a house. Angie quickly darted next to the car and peered into the trunk. Sadly, whatever had once been in the trunk had already been looted, with the only thing remaining being a couple of plastic grocery bags and an empty two-liter bottle, which had once held soda. Dejected, Angie moved to the next car down the street, an orange Chevrolet Silverado pickup truck.

The bed of the pickup truck was empty but the driver's door to the cab was open, so she climbed in and quickly searched through the extended cab. Under the passenger seat she found a small bag of marijuana which she quickly discarded, remembering her past as an honor student. Next to the bag, she discovered a small semi-automatic pistol. While she despised guns, she was familiar enough with them to know how to use one and how to check the magazine. Upon determining that the magazine was full, and that a round was chambered, she ensured that the safety was on, before slipping the small pistol into her right pants pocket.

Happy that she had found a weapon, even if it was only a marginal one, she slipped out of the truck and made her way to the next vehicle on the street, a red Mustang. She almost squealed with delight, when two grocery bags were spotted in the back seat. But she remembered her noise-discipline and instead just smiled broadly. She glanced around nervously, before reaching her hand down and quietly lifting the door handle. As the door opened, the interior light blazed on, appearing as a small sun in the otherwise dark neighborhood.

Angie cursed as she quickly grabbed both of the grocery bags before she gently pushed the car door closed. As she prepared to make her escape, she was frightened by a voice from behind her, which instructed her to drop the bags and turn around.

The bags crashed to the ground and partially buried themselves into the snow, which was covering the ground. Angie slowly turned around to face the aggressor. She noticed a large, middle-aged, bearded man, who was holding a large knife. She guessed that it might have been a bayonet, although she'd never actually seen a bayonet before. Angie pleaded with the man to just keep the groceries and let her go. But instead, he laughed maniacally.

The man told her that he would let her go, but only after satisfying her, promising her a night that she'd never forget. With that, he began unbuckling his belt, as he commanded her to also remove her pants. Angie dropped her hands to her belt and began fumbling with the buckle with her left hand. However, she slipped her right hand into her pants pocket and withdrew the small pistol. She quickly flipped the safety off and pointed it in the man's direction, before pulling the trigger multiple times. *POP-POP-POP-POP-POP!*

The man glanced down at his chest which was covered with several holes, each of which was bleeding profusely, with the dark red blood staining the man's white tee-shirt. He glanced up at Angie and took two steps, before his brown eyes rolled up. With that, he collapsed into a heap on the ground. Angie wasted no time flicking the small pistol's safety back on and stashed it back in her pants pocket. She realized that the gunshots would attract unwanted attention, so she then grabbed the two bags of groceries and ran as fast as her feet would carry her.

After several blocks of running, mostly zigzagging between burned buildings, she slipped into an open garage and collapsed. She started shivering uncontrollably, although she really wasn't sure if it was due to the cold, exhaustion, or the fact that she had just killed a man. After many minutes, she got her breathing under control and slipped back out of the garage. She gave the place where she had shot the man a wide berth, as she made her way out of the town and back to the toolshed she shared with her half-sister.

When she arrived back at the toolshed, after having taken another diversion to confuse anyone who was trying to follow her tracks through the snow, she gasped in horror as she saw the door standing open. She poked her head inside and looked for her sister, but the shed was empty. Her first thought was that someone had broken into the shed and abducted her sister. But as she examined the door, she could find no evidence that it had been forced open. Next, she checked the hiding spot for the key to the door and found the key still in its secret location. She examined the snow around the shed and found many sets of footprints, but there appeared to be only two sizes: her size and a smaller size.

As she spun in circles, looking for additional clues, she was ecstatic to see her sister leaving the nearby woods, with an armload of downed branches and twigs. Angie stomped her foot and pointed into the shed. She waited until Lisa had made her way inside, before she retrieved the key, picked up the bags of groceries and followed her inside. Once inside, she closed and locked the door before turning and glaring at Lisa in the dim light provided by the makeshift stove.

Why, she wondered, were 16-year-old girls so irresponsible? She remembered when she had been 16 years old and how responsible she had been. She'd been an honor student in high school and had planned on attending college to get a degree to become a veterinarian. Lisa, on the other hand, was a poor student who seemed to enjoy using her looks to achieve popularity.

Angie's emotions overflowed. She was happy that her sister was safe and that she had two whole bags of groceries. Yet, she was disappointed with Lisa for taking a chance on scavenging firewood, with no idea of the dangers involved, nor a weapon. And, she was fraught with angst about having killed a man, a man who had been intending to perform evil acts on her. As the tears flowed down her face, Lisa was oblivious to her grief and happily chattered about the groceries and the firewood she had obtained.

Content to just sit on the edge of the cot and allow the tears to flow, Angie finally relaxed a bit. Then, ever the intellectual, she wondered whether killing the evil man had made it too dangerous to scavenge in the town. Did the man have friends who would miss him? Would they come looking for what had happened to their friend and try to track down the person who had done it? Did she and Lisa need to abandon the toolshed? But if they were to abandon the toolshed, where would they go? Shelter was one of the necessities for survival and the sad fact was that there were very few suitable shelters, especially given the frigid winter weather which was plaguing the area.

Angie briefly considered loading up their meager supplies into the scavenged shopping cart and heading away from the town on the narrow country road which was in front of the burned farmhouse. But despite having grown up in the neighboring town she was not familiar with the geography of the area. She wasn't sure how far it was to the next town, or what was beyond that. And, she certainly wasn't sure what kind of shelter she could find for the pair of them. She wondered whether it would be better to stay and fight anyone who found them, or whether it would be better to take a chance on dying from exposure by leaving the area.

About the Author — Albert B. Moss

Mr. Moss lives on a small farm in the foothills of the Appalachian Mountains, in northeastern Kentucky, with his devoted horse, who he rescued from a kill-pen, three days before it was due to be sent to slaughter. When he's not working on the farm, or writing post-apocalyptic stories, he works, remotely, for a large multi-national company as a cryptographer. His degrees are in electrical engineering, although he has 15 years of experience as a computer programmer, and 20 years of experience as a cryptographer.

CHAPTER 4 — TIPPING

Lacey sniffed, wishing for the millionth time that she had soft, aloe-infused tissues to wipe her nose with and not a rough piece of grey rag. Her nose was becoming sore and red-raw with cold. Dragging the coarse cloth over it was not helping matters.

Not that she even knew what aloe was; not really. Her mother used to tell her about such things, talking to her of what she called the 'old world' when she tucked her in at night. Lacey would curl up under layers of musty-smelling blankets and listen; watching her mother become wistful, her voice full of loss and regret as she talked of the years before Lacey was born. Sometimes, when Lacey was just on the sleepy edge of oblivion, she thought she heard her mother crying.

Lacey hadn't been tucked in at night for a while now. The only time her mother accompanied her to bed was when she admitted to being afraid of shadows, or when she swore, she had seen something lurching and dragging its way up the street beyond her window.

Lacey had never seen a zombie either. Her mother rarely talked about them, but when she did, Lacey could sense the fear in her words, see the tension in her face.

"All that was over and done with a year or two before you came along. There are no zombies anymore," her mother would say, brushing the matter aside. Then she would help Lacey into bed before kissing her on her forehead and turning to look out of the window anyway, just in case.

Lacey was thirteen today. A big girl now. No need for all the reassurances of childhood anymore. She was 'growing up fast' as her mother had said only that morning.

She didn't feel very grown up.

She didn't feel very much like it was her birthday, either. In years past, her mother had managed to scrape together some kind of treat to mark the day. Times were harder and leaner now. Lacey didn't hold out much hope of any kind of sweet treat that evening.

As if all that wasn't bad enough, her mother had sent her out tipping. She trudged along through the slushy, ankle-deep snow, feeling the biting cold even through her ancient boots. The icy pain in her toes added to her misery. She trod gloomily on, head down, dragging the sack behind her. Not so long ago, she knew, the tip would have been the last place anyone would have willingly gone to. It had been a place of death and danger; her mother had once revealed — a place where bodies piled up. Where rats and disease lurked. Where the dregs of humankind once met to conspire. As if humanity hadn't been through enough already.

Not anymore. These days, it was nothing more than a huge pile of slowly decomposing waste — except for the plastic, of course. Plastic jugs, cups, buckets, anything of that sort was to be collected and brought home. There was no one to make plastic anymore, so such things were prized.

The rats were still there, but they had learned to keep a distance from humans. Rats had been hunted for meat enough times to have taught them a lesson, it seemed.

It would be Christmas soon. Her mother had told her that it was a religious holiday. She hadn't gone into details and Lacey hadn't cared to pursue it. She was more interested in recounts of lavish dinners, sweets and chocolates, brightly colored decorations, and prettily wrapped gifts beneath the Christmas tree.

That was the thing that gripped her imagination the most: a Christmas tree. It sounded like a wonderful thing. Think of it! A tree, indoors, all covered in baubles, berries and shining, twinkling lights. "Like the night stars," her mother had said, "except they were all different colors, not just gold or silver."

Lost in her daydreaming, Lacey came to a sudden halt when she realized she was almost at the tip. It was a dark, dismal day, the sky full of snow yet to fall. She sniffed again, patting at her nose tentatively with the rag.

"You out tipping then?"

Lacey turned, dismayed to see Howie and Philip coming up behind her. They were twins, two years younger than her and a continuous pain, as far as Lacey was concerned. She had expressed this thought to her mother once.

"Those two remind me of Ronnie and Reggie," her mother had said, offering no further explanation, leaving Lacey mystified. Her mother had seen her look of puzzlement and said, "Look, all I am saying is don't bother with them if you don't have to Lacey, okay?"

"There are no other kids around here to play with," Lacey had replied contrarily, defending her right to befriend the twins even though seconds earlier she had been complaining about them.

Her mother's eyes were suddenly wet; bright with unspilled tears. Lacey had no idea why. For reasons she could not explain, it had made Lacey cross. She had turned and stalked away, stamping her feet.

Now, she intended to heed her mother's advice; she would have as little to do with these two as possible.

"What's it look like?" she snapped back, rolling her eyes at the stupidity of the question.

"All right, just asking," Howie said, grinning.

"Found anything good?" Philip asked, his warm breath curling white in the frigid air.

"I haven't even started yet, have I?"

"We have," Philip declared, "We found this!"

He pulled something from the back pocket of his trousers, waving it in the air wildly, "*First strike!*" he screeched girlishly.

Something hard and stinging slapped into Lacey's face. "Ow!" she exclaimed, raising a hand to her cheek.

"Ha-ha! Got you!" Philip danced about, his brother glaring at him.

"That's not fair!" Howie complained, "You

never said *'War's On!'* You've got to say *'War's On'* first, or else how do I know we've even started? You cheated!"

"I did not cheat! You're just annoyed because I won!" Philip declared, still waving the object around, it glinting silver in the dim light.

Annoyed, Lacey reached out a hand to grab his wrist, stopping him mid-wave. She ignored his outrage as she snatched the thing out of his hand.

"A serving spoon?" she said, "You hit me with a serving spoon! What is this stupid game you're playing anyway?"

"It's called *'War's On,'*" Howie explained, "except Philip doesn't play fair, do you Philip? You're supposed to shout, *'War's On'* before you do *'First Strike.'* That's the rules!" He turned an accusing eye on his brother, who shrugged carelessly.

"Rules are for breaking," Philip said, for a split-second appearing much older than his eleven years. The impression vanished with his next words.

"Anyway, *War's On!*" he yelled, snatching back the serving spoon before dashing away.

Distracted, Lacey was too slow to stop Howie's attack. He watched his brother flee, then shrieked the words *'First strike!'*

Something hard and painful slapped into her cheek for a second time. She screamed, more from rage than hurt, while lunging to get her hands on Howie. He was too fast, ducking away, laughing exaggeratedly as he clutched at what looked like a rusty, misshapen whisk.

The boys disappeared from view. Lacey did not have the will to chase after them, but if they were stupid enough to come within grabbing distance again, she would teach them a short, sharp lesson.

From nowhere, the image of Bear, sitting on the end of her bed, popped into her mind. She had loved that cuddly toy when she was small. As she grew older, she had studied its face more closely, understanding that it was a lopsided, even strange looking thing. The eyes were two different colors, one hanging much lower on its cheek than the other. Its nose was half-missing, its sewn-on mouth was stuck in an eternal pout.

Lacey sniffed again, loudly. If Howie or Philip came near her once more today, their faces would look like Bear's by the time she finished with them. Except that Bear's pallor was a shade of brown. Howie and Philip's faces would be a nice purplish-blue, due to bruising.

She decided she would put Bear away when she got home, the thought of that crooked, leering face watching her when she was asleep suddenly made her uneasy. She was thirteen today after all. Too old now for cuddly toys.

She stepped into the tip and began climbing one of the mounds of detritus. When she reached the top she paused, looking out at the scene before her. There were similar mounds as far as the eye could see; some smaller, some larger. It was like looking across a panorama of small hills and valleys. Covered in snow, they even managed to look almost pretty. Her mother had told her it was just as well they didn't know what was right at the bottom of those piles and warned her not to burrow down too far when she went tipping.

Two tracks of footprints showed her which way

the twins had taken. Resolved, she hefted the sack clear of the snow and set off in the opposite direction.

The going was soft underfoot. She kept sliding downwards, even though she was placing her feet at an angle, effectively walking sideways, as she walked up and down the piles of rubbish. She was painfully aware that there were sharp things lurking under the deceiving snow and was careful not to fall. Here and there, bits of things poked out, ruining the clean white image. Lacey inspected them briefly, finding nothing of any worth.

Despite the cold, Lacey began to sweat inside her coat. The constant trudging was hard work, making her hot. She stopped to catch her breath, leaning against a fence post for support.

She hadn't realized how far she had come. This was a part of the tip that was new to her. Even better, there were no tell-tale footprints heralding the presence of the twins, or anyone else. She had it all to herself.

Encouraged by the thought that there might be new treasures to discover here, Lacey pressed on. The mounds here were arranged in a rough circle, a clear, flat space in the center of them. Lacey stepped into it, the hairs on the back of her neck rising, her senses suddenly alert.

It felt like she was being watched. Like there were eyes on her. Lacey shuddered, putting the thought aside. No one was watching her; it was simply that she was in an unfamiliar place.

She took a few more steps into the clearing, her feet crunching in the snow. The feeling underfoot suddenly changed, having a springy sensation.

Puzzled, Lacey crouched low, took a trowel from the sack, and began to clear the snow away.

About three inches down, she found the explanation for the sponginess beneath her feet. She was standing on an old mattress. Amazed that it had not yet rotted through, she decided to try to go around it; there could well be some sharp, coiled springs hidden there, just waiting to catch her out.

There came the sudden, mad yell of 'War's On!' Lacey didn't know how the boys could have come so close without her knowing, but she was determined not to fall victim to them again.

She spun around, trying to judge which way they would come from. There was no obvious sign of movement. She couldn't hear them giggling or whispering like the little fools they were. She cursed under her breath; a word she knew her mother definitely would not approve of even though Lacey had heard her mutter it under her breath herself when she was exasperated. Where were they?

Lacey crossed the clearing, exiting on the other side, all thoughts of searching for buried treasure gone.

She came out into another clearing, empty of all signs of life. She crossed it quickly, stopping to cock her head and listen at one point, when she thought she heard crying.

She was right. Someone was definitely crying, a quiet sobbing, as if afraid. Something told Lacey to proceed with caution.

She chose to find a way between two mounds rather than climb one and announce her presence to whoever must be on the other side. This way, there was a possibility she might not be seen. Not immediately, anyway.

She crept through the gap as quietly as she could, lifting the sack rather than dragging it. What she saw made her catch her breath. She had to take a moment to understand what she was looking at.

Philip was standing with his back to her, hopping back and forth from one foot to the other, his glee evident even from behind. He had the whisk in his right hand, the serving spoon in the other. For some inexplicable reason, his brother Howie was on his knees in front of him, his hands apparently fastened behind his back.

Lacey watched, horrified. Each time Philip changed feet, he slapped one of the utensils into Howie's face. Now and then he would shout, *"War's on!"* followed by, *"First strike!"* Then he would begin battering Howie's face afresh. Howie, bloodied, distressed, and crying, gave no sign of having seen Lacey arrive.

She had to do something. As much as she had been keen to get revenge on the twins earlier… she had never imagined harm like this. This felt odd, in a very bad way. She had to stop it.

Hoping she would sound as much as possible like her mother when she was truly annoyed, Lacey stood tall and straight. She took a deep breath and said, "And just what do you think you are doing?"

To her amazement, it worked. Philip whirled around, dropping the whisk and spoon into the snow as if they were suddenly afire. Guilt was written all over his face.

"I didn't mean it!" He said hurriedly, unaware of the absurdity of his words. Behind him, Howie sagged in relief.

"Of course, you meant it, you idiot!" Lacey snapped, "You don't accidentally tie someone up and start hitting them in the face with kitchen implements!" She had to stop there; afraid she would burst out laughing. It sounded so stupid when she said it out loud. She bit her lip, not wanting Philip to think he was off the hook because she was smiling.

"What have you tied him up with, anyway?" She demanded, approaching the boys.

A look of alarm came into Philip's face. "It's only a game," he protested as Lacey made her way round, behind Howie, "It'll be my turn next. He can tie me up, right Howie?"

Howie said nothing, tears running down his cheeks, mixing with the blood there, falling into the snow in red droplets.

"Oh my God!" Lacey said when she saw what was wrapped around Howie's wrists. Her features contorted into shock and revulsion, she looked up at Philip. "What is *wrong* with you?"

She fell to her knees, carefully and slowly releasing Howie of the twists of barbed wire that had made him his brother's prisoner. They both looked up and froze when Philip roared his reply.

"There's nothing wrong with me!" He insisted, "Dad is always saying that! So is your mum! So is everybody, but it's all of you who are wrong, not me!" He was raging, his throat raw with cold and effort.

Lacey finished releasing Howie, seeing pricks of blood where the barbed wire had dug in. He didn't thank her, or even look at her. He just began scooping up handfuls of snow and laying them against his cheeks, seeking to cool the swollen, inflamed skin there.

Lacey left him to it. She stood again, very deliberately brandishing the trowel like a weapon, knowing with absolute certainty that she would use it if she had to. This didn't feel like a game gone too far. This felt like something else altogether.

Philip pretended not to notice the trowel, though she saw his quick glance downwards. He was breathing hard, willing himself to calm down. His thin shoulders rose and fell as he took in shallow, tight breaths of air.

"It really was just a game, honestly," he insisted forlornly, "It just went a bit too far, like it does sometimes. We don't have to tell anyone, do we? We can just keep it our secret, right?"

For the second time that day, Philip all at once appeared much older than his years. It made Lacey even more uncomfortable. She shivered involuntarily.

"I don't believe in secrets," she said. Not her mother's words this time. This pearl of wisdom was all her own. She suspected her mother kept a great deal of secrets; things about the past she did not want Lacey to know—like who, or where her father was. She was thirteen today, a big girl now. When she got home, she would sit her mother down and say those very same words to her, *"I don't believe in secrets."* Time her mother stopped treating her like a child.

"So, what then?" Philip asked, a wicked little glint in his eye, "What are you going to do, Lacey? What's any of this got to do with you?"

Lacey hesitated, unsure. What was she going to do? What did it have to do with her?

"It's just wrong, that's all," she started, "You can't go around tying people up with barbed wire! I mean, don't you understand how wrong that is? How are you going to explain the state of his face when you get home?"

Philip shrugged sulkily, "We can say he slid down a pile, scraped his face on something sharp," he offered.

Next to her, Howie was at last getting to his feet, the legs of his trousers plastered in snow.

"This game of yours; this ridiculous '*War's On.*' It has to stop," Lacey went on.

"Who are you? Our mum?" Howie asked, trudging his way round to stand alongside his brother.

Lacey's jaw dropped in astonishment. "Are you serious?" she asked Howie, disbelieving, "Two minutes ago you were sobbing in fear and pain because of what he was doing to you and now you're on his side?"

"Of course, I am! He's my brother. I am always on his side."

"Even when barbed wire is slicing into your wrists and he is cutting your cheeks open with a serving spoon?"

Howie's bottom lip stuck out, tears standing in his eyes. He nodded a reply, wiping his face with the back of his hand. Philip gave her a smug smile.

"Unbelievable!" she announced at last, "Okay, fine. Kill each other for all I care. That's the last time I help either of you."

Unwilling to turn her back, she began to march past them, back the way she had come. As she drew level, Philip turned to her, raising the whisk as he began to shout his strange little battle cry; *'War's On, First Stri....'*

The look she gave him stopped the boy dead, the words fading on his lips. At thirteen, Lacey was a good head and shoulders taller than the twins, much heavier set, too. Yet she could see they were going to end up both taller and far stronger than she was. If she were ever going to set the twins straight, it would have to be now.

"I'll have those!" she said, plucking the whisk and the spoon from Philip's hands, "If either of you dare touch me again, if you ever dare try your pathetic little *'War's On'* game with me, or any other kind of stupid, little boy game again, I will make you very, very sorry," she warned. She saw that she was waving the trowel under Philip's nose. He had lost some of his bravado. His eyes wide and boyish again as he leaned back to avoid the implement. Behind him, Howie sniffed desolately, his face swelling rapidly.

Lacey relented, alarmed. She tried to maintain her air of threat, not wanting to show the boys that she had frightened herself almost as much as she had scared them. Not taking her eyes off them until she had reached the gap between the mounds, she was gratified to see that they both looked more than a little cowed.

She ducked around the mound with a huge sigh of relief. She wished the wretched twins had not ventured out today. Some birthday this was turning out to be.

She trudged home, making only a token effort at searching for loot. She stumbled across a box of plastic pegs at one point, excitedly squeezing one open only to find it snapped before it was even fully extended. The same was true of the others. Dispirited, Lacey kicked the box back into the snow. At least she had a whisk and a spoon for her efforts. Her mother didn't have to know how she came by them.

There was smoke drifting from the chimney by the time she had stepped back onto the street. It had started snowing again, growing heavier by the minute. Lacey passed the rusted, crumbling shells of what her mother had told her were cars. It was hard to picture the street busy with these vehicles up and down all the time, all shiny and new. Everything about the Old World was hard for Lacey to imagine. All she had ever known was the abandoned, old, and crumbling. The scavenging, stealing, and surviving. Sometimes her mother talked about the world getting back to the way it used to be, once the human race rallied round again.

She talked about it less and less these days, Lacey noticed.

She turned into the house that was their current home. Her mother had been surprised when they found it empty, though there were signs that others had used it before them. The door was intact, still fitted its frame and could be barred from the inside; someone had added that, her mother said. The fireplace was usable, there were even beds in the upstairs rooms though they had to improvise for mattresses. All in all, they were lucky to have found such a place, her mother said. Who knew? Maybe they would stay there for good this time.

Lacey pushed open the door, knowing her mother would not lock it while she was gone. She slipped the wooden bar into place, grateful to be out of the snow. Hurriedly she removed her wet coat and hat, kicked off her spiteful, freezing boots, and made her way to the only room where they had a fire lit; the kitchen.

Her mother was sitting expectantly at the table, a furtive smile playing about her lips. She greeted Lacey warmly, bidding her sit by the fire. She did no more than nod approval at the kitchen implements Lacey set on the table.

"I've got something for you," her mother said, sliding a parcel across the table, "Happy birthday, Lacey!"

Surprised, Lacey reached for the parcel. She recognized the paper it was wrapped in; her mother had torn a strip from the wallpaper in what had once been the living room. It was peeling from the walls, was probably easy to take down.

Faded patterns of birds and flowers adorned the paper. Lacey smiled; it was still pretty, despite everything. She looked across at her mother, unsure.

"Go on," her mother encouraged her. "Open it."

Lacey peeled away the paper. It had not been fastened in any way, just tucked around the gift inside. A soft bundle lay beneath the wrapping. Lacey picked it up, watching it fall away to make one long strip of loosely knitted wool. A scarf.

"Thank you!" Lacey breathed, genuinely pleased, "But where did you get it?"

"I didn't get it, I made it," her mother said proudly, "Finger knitted it. When we first came here, I found an old jumper at the back of the drawers in the main bedroom. It must have fallen down there when the people who lived here moved out,"

"Or when they were looted," Lacey added. Her mother frowned.

"Anyway, it was such a pretty shade of pink that I knew then and there that I would hide it from you to make a gift. I could have just given you the jumper I suppose, but I wanted you to have something that was really from me. Do you know what I mean?"

"I do Mother, thank you," Lacey said. She wrapped the scarf about her neck, enjoying its warmth and softness.

"Thirteen today! I can hardly believe it. My little girl, all grown up!"

Lacey gripped the ends of the scarf with both hands, considering. This was such a rare, warm moment, such a real treat to have an actual gift. She didn't want to do or say anything to spoil it.

Her mother was at the fire, stirring a pan of some broth she had concocted. Lacey had long since learned not to ask what was in it. Her stomach growled appreciatively at the smell.

"I bumped into Howie and Philip," Lacey began tentatively.

"Those two! Nothing but trouble," her mother sneered.

"Yes," Lacey agreed, her thoughts drifting, remembering what she had resolved regarding secrets.

"Mother, I don't mean to be rude, but I think I should tell you that I don't really believe in secrets," she said, her voice quavering.

Her mother straightened, turning to look at her, "Oh?"

"No," Lacey confirmed, "I don't think I do. So, I have some questions for you; if you have the time?"

Her mother looked all at once defeated. She sat at the table opposite Lacey, waiting.

"First of all," Lacey asked, her face solemn, "Who are Ronnie and Reggie?"

Her mother's reaction surprised her. First, she sighed in obvious relief. Then, she burst out laughing.

It took her a long time to stop.

About the Author — S._P. Oldham

S P Oldham is married with two grown up children and an adorable Cocker Spaniel named Milo. She lives in the beautiful Sirhowy Valley in South Wales. She has always enjoyed writing and has recently ventured into self-publishing. Although she has published mainly horror and dark fiction, she likes to dabble in other genres from time to time. She is also an avid reader.

Find her on Amazon https://www.amazon.com/S-P-Oldham/e/B01N2LSUMX

CHAPTER 5 —THE PROMISE

It had been a miserable six months. Clive Martin was headed home after another mandatory twelve-hour shift at the county jail.

When was my last day off? Had it been over four months? Holy crap! I'm so tired! Well, I won't be employed after today. Screw it. My family and my health are more important than the risks associated with traveling the twelve miles between my home and work every day. I wasn't going to break a promise to my kids. I'm so pissed!

He was informed at the end of his shift tonight that he had to work on Christmas day. He'd been strung along for weeks and was repeatedly told they 'would do their best' to honor his request. He'd taken Christmas week off every year since his kids were born. They'd already put up and decorated the Christmas tree and he had promised them he'd be home for Christmas. It was only four days away. Given the amount of horror and tragedy they'd experienced they needed Christmas to be as normal as it could be. They deserved it.

He'd received 'IOUs' from the county for his

last four paychecks. He was supposed to get direct deposit paychecks twice a month. Of course, the county kept telling employees they'd 'take care of the loyal ones' who stuck it out until the recovery. No one knew what that meant. It had been over six months! The county had arranged a deal with a bank that would cash the IOUs for the employees. It was one of those banks that were considered to be 'too big to fail.' The bank had made the employees sign a bunch of legal paperwork, forcing everyone to give them forty-nine percent of the IOUs. *Disgusting vultures!* The bank ended up taking possession of the IOU, giving fifty-one percent of the value to the employee in cash, and when the county eventually makes good on the IOU... the bank will collect the entire check. So, in addition to paying what he called the government's increased 'panic taxes.' AKA theft, as a response to the failing economy, the bank was fleecing him and his co-workers who just wanted to keep their houses and feed their families.

What was left of his paycheck barely kept his family fed and paid the mortgage—barely. What it certainly didn't do was pay for gasoline. At nearly $25 a gallon, gas was a luxury at this point which was why Clive was walking home with his trusty 18-speed Huffy mountain bike. When the poop hit the fan and major roads and bridges weren't safe enough for vehicles, he rescued it from the side of the house where the weeds and spider webs had swallowed it. He had spent hours taking it apart, cleaning it, lubricating it, and ensuring everything worked. Luckily, the local Wally-World had the right sized innertubes to fit the tires. They had seven left. He bought them all before prices skyrocketed along with several patch kits and a small bicycle repair kit.

Thirty-three years in the same career is pretty rare for a Gen-X'er like me. Nowadays these Gen-Y's or millennials had had three or four careers by the time they reach twenty-five. Don't get me started on Gen-Z's.

Born in 1972, most of his high school friends and similarly aged co-workers had already had three or four different careers in their lifetime. Either people had a hard time finding something they liked and were fulfilled by or they got bored way to easily. His dearly departed Grandfather who'd fought in WWII always had a rather negative view of life. He would simply scowl and say these younger generations were lazy and afraid to work hard at something long enough to be successful. He didn't really understand it himself, but to each his own! *We all forge our own path and are responsible for our successes and failures.*

Clive? He'd always wanted to be in some kind of law enforcement since the big career day event at his high school. The football field was packed goal to goal with tables and canopies set-up. Employers provided information pamphlets, pens, peachy folders and other free trinkets like key chains and soda pop covers to keep your drinks cool. Many military and law enforcement agencies were there. Men and women in crisp clean uniforms looked tough, professional, and prepared for anything. They looked like warriors. He remembered how they had made him feel safe. He wanted to be a warrior.

All military branches and most LE agencies in the county performed some sort of mock scene or scenario. There were swat teams, K-9 units, Humvees with .50 caliber machine guns, bomb squads, and hostage negotiation teams... all showing off their state-of-the-art equipment, guns, and tactics. They shot blanks out of their guns during these demonstrations! He chuckled to himself. The 80's were so different. Given the high number of mass shootings at schools that were happening across the nation prior to the great quake and collapse, there was no way an event like that would be allowed nowadays. For a young man seeking adventure in an exciting career it was the perfect career event. He'd found his calling. It was what he was meant to do.

Clive had liked his job. He'd enjoyed the people he had worked with, although most of them have left now. He had been good at it. He was sad to be leaving, and sometimes had been overwhelmed by the feelings of guilt for abandoning his co-workers. But Clive's family, friends, and neighbors needed him at home. They needed him alive. He had hung on longer than some but not as long as some others and hoped the ones he'd be leaving behind would be okay.

Things were getting worse in our nation every day. Death as a result of starvation, accident, weather, disease, or assault, was a real and constant threat. People were burying their loved ones in their backyards for Christ's sake!

It was December 21, 2021 at about 4:30 am. About six months after the great quake and collapse. Clive had just finished his shift and was walking north on the west side of the five-lane main road that went through the city. He was thinking of his family and reflecting on his lifelong commitment to serving his community, as a corrections deputy with the local sheriff's office, as he trudged towards home in the half-rain, half-sleet. It was pelting him due to the sideways, driving wind.

This was typical winter weather in most parts of western Washington. The city of Everett was known for getting more rain and snow than the surrounding cities even though it was at or near sea level, literally. Naval Station Everett was only a couple miles from the county jail where he worked. Everett was one of the most modern naval bases in the U.S.A., hosting aircraft carriers such as the USS Abraham Lincoln and a variety of other ships in the battle group. Everett was located in what the weather experts called "the convergence zone." This was what supposedly made the weather more unusual there.

The morning's weather was going to make Clive's trip home almost unbearable. Luckily, he had his Carhartt Dry Harbor weatherproof pants and jacket on, which kept him dry. His ECCO Rugged Track GTX boots that he'd been wearing as part of his work uniform doubled as a rain resistant hiking shoe and was the most comfortable, reliable boot he'd ever worn. Standing for hours on concrete floors and routinely having to run towards emergencies for decades had allowed him to experiment with a lot of footwear. Additionally, and most importantly, the knowledge that he'd be home in a little over an hour hugging his wife Holly of 18 years, his 15-year-old daughter Abigail, and his 11-year-old son Cayden, was what really kept him warm and drove him to get home quickly and safely. Although, he had serious doubts on the whole safely part.

Broadway Avenue and the surrounding blocks

had been known for its thriving businesses, fast food joints, minor league hockey and baseball teams, community college, historic theatre, and downtown area. And, of course, the pretty hanging flower baskets on the streetlights.

Unfortunately, it was also known for its gangs, drugs, and prostitution. In the last couple of years Clive had seen more SODA, stay out of drug area, orders issued to inmates who were making their way through the judicial system than he'd seen in his entire career. None of these orders did anything to actually reduce crime or the recidivism. They only resulted in a day or two in jail and fines which were never paid. The system had no teeth anymore. Addiction was a terrible thing and there just wasn't enough money, or common sense, to truly have an impact on the epidemic. It was sad really. Clive and his colleagues just kept seeing the same sickly, down on your luck, mentally ill, addicted folks booked into the jail repeatedly. Oh sure, there was that rare case once in a while, when someone completely turned their life around, but those were far and few in between and it wasn't 'the system' that got them there, but the tenacity and support of family and friends — and the addict's decision to finally do something positive.

About a month ago, while heading to work, Clive was riding his bike on this same street but heading south. He had seen a small group of homeless druggies sitting on the sidewalk. They had all their camping gear spread out and were blocking about twenty-five yards of sidewalk. It was a rare dry and sunny day in November. They were taking advantage of the warmth and "drying" their wet clothing, sleeping bags, and other items by laying them out. Clive got off his bike and walked around them by going into the street. He wasn't too worried about getting run over because 90% of the vehicles that used to be on the roads weren't anymore. He was, however, worried about getting robbed by those desperate junkies. He had decent clothes, nice boots, a bike with a luggage rack and milk crate zip tied to the back, and a backpack. Desperate times create desperate people. Clive had learned since the quake and the following collapse, that even the most harmless looking people can turn aggressively violent in an instant.

As he approached, he lifted the hem of his zip up fleece hoody over his HK Compact USP .40 handgun, tucking it in between his right hip and the pistol. This would give him quicker access to it just in case he needed it. It also made the gun visible to the group as he walked by. Although Clive was six-foot-two, 210 lbs., and in really good shape since having to bike 24 miles every day, he was hoping the open carry would be enough of a deterrent to any would be muggers in the group. It was.

Open carry had been legal in Washington for decades. But after rampant violence, including rapes and murders, had begun increasing throughout the state, some liberal politician pushed a law through the legislature quickly outlawing it. When he'd heard about the new law, Clive's first thought was that common sense was dead. He believed the law was the typical knee-jerk dumb foolery used by politicians who knew little to nothing about guns or self-defense.

Most left-leaning people just inherently believed that guns were dangerous and evil. They had convinced themselves that they were the leading authority on such subjects, despite their ignorance. There was no convincing them otherwise. *Let's make the law abiding citizens hide their evil guns so they can't hurt anyone*, Clive thought as he shook his head. Those politicians were clueless and had no idea how truly unintelligent they sounded. It just seemed to him that there was other, more important legislation that these highly paid politicians could be spending their time and effort on. Clive rarely, if ever, practiced open carry anyway, because he didn't want to draw unnecessary attention to himself, but there were certainly times when it was appropriate, like now. Ironically, those anti-gun politicians were always well-protected by highly skilled bodyguards who carried lots of scary guns.

Clive controlled his bike with his left hand and picked up his pace. As he passed the group, he saw a couple of them passed out with homemade tourniquets still wrapped around their arms with needles sticking out of veins. The worst part, which completely broke his heart, was seeing a little blonde girl sitting next to her mother who was 'sleeping.' She appeared to be four or five years old, dirty, stringy hair and no shoes. She had streams of mucus running down over her lips and down her chin. She was playing with a small stuffed bear which was missing an eye. It was just as filthy as she was.

Clive made it to work and immediately called the numbers for: DSHS, Department of Social & Health Services; CPS, Child Protective Services; and the EPD, Everett Police Department. He left messages detailing what he saw, where, and when. Most government agencies were overwhelmed and understaffed. This was due to the damage from the great quake that happened in late May, which was quickly followed by an economic collapse. Clive doubted that anyone ever went to check on the little girl. The group was gone when he headed home 13 hours later. It made him very thankful for his family and what they had.

Many law enforcement personnel had increasingly gone AWOL in the last couple of months. They wanted to take care of their families or move to a safer place away from the coast. Additionally, due to insane liberal policies and anti-police rhetoric coming from most democrats, the job was just too dangerous. Anyone with a uniform, even security guards, were being targeted in drive-by shootings and other random attacks. Death had been, and continued to be, an everyday occurrence since May for law enforcement personnel as well as citizens. Most LE agencies were down 70-percent of normal staffing levels. Anytime a loved one ventured out of their home it was of genuine concern whether they would ever come back. The concern and risks were even higher for those in uniform.

Luckily for Clive he didn't have to put on his uniform until he was inside the secure portion of the jail. His 'patrol' area was inside the walls, not outside on the street. He even got into the habit of washing and drying his uniform at work in the staff locker room so he wouldn't get caught with it out on the street. If some random mugger or gang member managed to get the drop on him found evidence in Clive's backpack that he worked in law enforcement, it would surely result in his death. Clive had no doubt about that.

The dangers were just as real inside the jail. All non-violent felony and misdemeanor criminals had been released months ago and the majority of the inmate housing units were now closed and empty. That left only the worst of society still incarcerated. These were people with little or nothing to lose, and who placed no value on life except their own. A rookie deputy had nearly lost his life last week after getting stabbed several times by a homemade shank. The inmate had made the weapon out of a serving spoon. The serving spoon was plastic and had easily been shaped and sharpened by rubbing it on the concrete floor.

Throughout the city gangs roved around in packs terrorizing the innocent. Closet serial rapists and murderers snuck around like ninjas, taking advantage, in a world without rule of law. Cops were simply reactionary for the most part. There weren't enough of them and only the most serious of crimes like rape, murder, and serious assaults, were responded to. 'Responded to' meant sometime within the next 24 hours — if you were lucky. There weren't enough police available to actually investigate and arrest anyone. They simply took reports and archived them in the hopes that after the nation recovered, they could track down the criminals and hold them accountable.

His thoughts of murder and rape suddenly snapped Clive out of his reminiscing and inner thoughts. He looked at his watch. It was only 0445 hours! He was a bit surprised he'd only left work fifteen minutes ago. His watch was always set to display military time. A habit born out of his chosen career and from writing thousands of reports. He reminded himself that even though most folks were asleep at this time of morning, a portion of Everett's criminal element probably wasn't. He needed to be alert and aware of his surroundings. He chastised himself for such a stupid mistake.

He'd only walked about three-quarters of a mile since he'd left work. The weather was slowing him down. He needed to pick up the pace. As he pushed on, he noticed that he could see his breath emanating from him in rapid, bright puffs of condensation. He worried this would draw unwanted attention. He briefly stopped, looked around, and listened for about 30 seconds. It was amazing how quiet the world had become since a lot of the machinery, vehicles, HVAC units, and other gadgets we took for granted stop being used. He felt his senses had become more acute, but it was probably just that they had much less noise to filter through. He heard nothing but a dog barking. It was faint and far off.

He leaned his bike against his hip so he could pull his olive drab shemagh up over his mouth and nose. This would minimize the visible condensation coming from his breath. His kids teased him all the time about his "tacti-scarf." He always explained to them the difference between an actual scarf and a shemagh just so they'd learn another lesson on how a shemagh could be used. Clive thought they teased him just to see what else their dad could come up with.

His son Cayden participated in the teasing until he got a "tacti-scarf" of his own for his birthday last year. Cayden was born on a cold day on New Year's Eve, so the gift seemed appropriate. He had always been Clive's little buddy. Cayden looked up to Clive and was overjoyed to get a cool "tacti-scarf" just like Dad's. He absolutely loved it and was now rarely seen without it anymore.

Clive took another look around. All was quiet except the rain and the wind pelting him, dripping off roofs and down gutters. In another mile he'd be coming up to the blocks that contained Providence Hospital and the community college to the west. The jail was in between Wall Street and Pacific Avenue. The roughly three miles between it and to the north, where Broadway turned into Highway 529, was the most dangerous part of his trek. Once he arrived at the 529 bridge, which spanned the Snohomish River, it immediately turned into farmland, sloughs, and industrial businesses. With the drastic decrease in human population the risk of being ambushed would go down and he would feel comfortable enough to get on his bike and make better time.

This three-mile stretch was what Clive called 'the gauntlet." Both the west and east sides of Broadway Avenue contained the city's desperate criminal element, therefore increasing the potential for a sudden violent encounter. Clive had run countless scenarios through his mind during his trips back and forth to work. He always wanted to have the tactical advantage if approached or attacked. If he was on his bike, pedaling fast to get home quickly, and had to suddenly get off of it in order to seek cover, he could fall and injure himself. He could make unnecessary noise when he was not meaning to. By simply walking next to his bike he could quickly get off the road and hide, or immediately drop it in order to draw his firearm and use both hands.

In the last several months there had been plenty of times Clive thought he might not make it home. He'd had to hide and wait, take alternate routes to avoid trouble, and once, even came remarkably close to shooting someone. Each of these incidents provided him with an opportunity to learn. Clive always looked for ways to avoid a confrontation and using force. Each of these times he was delayed getting home, and Holly had been worried sick. Those who had working cell phones knew that they were unreliable at best. Forget about making calls. Texts would get through once in a while, but most people simply couldn't afford to pay their cell phone bills anymore. Clive's family didn't have cell service, so they rarely used their iPhones. They were $950 paper weights.

Clive was already starting to feel the cold bite into him, but he knew his merino wool socks, thermal underwear, fleece winter hiking pants, and the fleece zip up hoody under his rain gear, would keep him warm enough. He pressed on towards home. Another block down, another block closer to home. One foot in front of the other. He noticed the rain had lightened up a bit.

Clive was keenly aware of his surroundings, but it didn't stop him from thinking about his family. He couldn't wait to get back to them. Although he'd done this dozens of times since the quake and the collapse, this time was different. He didn't want to jinx it. It would be the last time he made this journey. Abigail's long strawberry blonde hair and freckled face, Cayden's dimpled grin and faux-hawk haircut, and Holly's curly hair and full lips flashed through his mind. He smiled.

The next mile and a half was slow going but thankfully uneventful. He'd stop when random opportunities for concealment would present themselves, listen for a short period, then continue on. Clive reached the 7-11 store that sat on the east side right across the street from the community college entrance. The store was boarded up, having been looted and burnt out from arson weeks ago. Scorch marks weaved their way up the sides of the small building. Next door to it was a Subway sandwich shop that didn't fare much better. Only about half of a mile left, to the bridge and safety. The sound of the wet grass and mud squishing out from under his boots was metronomic.

Suddenly, there was a noise off to the right about 20 yards ahead. A scuffling sound. Clive stopped, leaning the bike against his left hip, and drew his pistol. He'd been sticking to the far right, off the sidewalk, using the trees and bushes for concealment. He now stood behind a tree, but it was only about 12 inches wide. Not much cover but the only available.

He peered in the direction he'd heard the sound. He caught a brief glimpse of movement in between the two stores, where there was small five-foot-wide alley. He thought maybe it could have been an animal but then he smelled cigarette smoke. Stray cats don't smoke cigarettes. Adrenaline entered his system and his senses were heightened. He waited. Five minutes went by. Nothing. 10 minutes. The smell of smoke went away and there was no movement. 20 minutes now. He was getting cold and tired of holding his handgun. Both his hands were gripping the gun, pointing it at the threat area. He held it tucked in close to his ribcage in a weapons retention position.

Should he investigate? He weighed the risks of breaking cover; to either run and ride like the wind or investigate and confront whoever was there if necessary. The problem was he didn't know who was there or if they remained at this point... and he sure as hell couldn't outrun or outride a bullet. He'd have to take a look.

"Damn it!" he whispered.

He'd leaned his bike against the tree and then placed his backpack into his homemade rear bike basket. He'd decided he was going to go straight to the alley quickly and quietly. He pulled his SureFire G2x flashlight out of his pocket and used a classic Chapman technique; with his left hand supporting his right hand. The night sights on his H&K were easily obtained by his eyes. He bent his knees, took a deep breath, and quickly started walking, heel to toe, towards the alley. He turned on the flashlight and was covering the distance quickly. If he encountered someone, he'd engage them with maximum aggressive verbal command presence and, if necessary... immediate and violent action.

Ten yards down. Halfway there. The flashlight lit up the alley. He'd be able to see anyone who stepped out. Clive's gate was smooth and fast. By 'combat walking,' he was able to minimize the sway and bounce of his pistol. Should he need to acquire a target, he could do so quickly and accurately. Although his heart was pounding in his ears and his respiratory rate had increased, he felt calm. He'd decided, and he knew what he needed to do.

Five yards to go. He started pieing the corner to

the alley as he approached. He instinctively bent his knees some more to try to shrink himself as a target.

The second he cleared the corner he saw a plume of flame from the end of the alley about forty feet away. Strange, he didn't seem to hear a bang. Clive's mind was probably trying to block out the reality of the situation. He suddenly felt like he couldn't breath and then he was falling backwards. It took him a millisecond to comprehend what was happening. He was already halfway to the ground.

He realized that he'd been shot.

Still falling; a burning heat was spreading across his chest like he'd never felt before. He tried to suck in a gulp of air to no avail. His brain was telling his body to do something, and it just wasn't happening. His butt, then his back, then his head, hit the pavement. He felt his head make a thick cracking sound and he wondered how much it would bleed before he died? His vision began to fade. He felt light, cold sprinkles of rain dappling his face and envisioned them mixing with his tears. The last thing he saw was his flashlight skittering off to his left. He was so tired.

Clive was amazed he wasn't dead! He must have only blacked out for a second or two because when he opened his eyes, he noticed his flashlight was gently rocking back and forth. It was also miraculously pointing down the alley thereby lighting up his attacker. Although it went against everything he wanted to do at that moment, Clive held his breath and didn't move. There was so much pain! But, Clive had a secret. He'd requisitioned his Level IIIA+ soft body armor from his employer at the end of his last work shift and had no intention of returning it. He was wearing it now. He could feel his handgun resting in his right hand. *How had I not dropped it?* He wondered. He played possum as his attacker got closer. The older looking man was scroungy, wet, and dressed in rags. He had a wild look in his eye and a huge smile on his face, like he'd just bagged a ten-point buck or won the lottery. Clive caught a glint of silver in the man's right hand and the round shape of a cylinder. With a face so covered in long, matted beard and dirt Clive couldn't actually tell what nationality this scumbag was. *It doesn't matter.* Clive said to himself. The old man was not long for this world.

The would-be murderer cackled with joy as he got closer and yelled, "I got me a bike and backpack now! How you like dem' apples Mother?!"

The man foolishly squatted down near Clive's right leg, poking at the leg with his revolver. With a subtle canting of his wrist Clive quickly and efficiently angled his HK up and pulled the trigger five times. He had decided to 'stich' his attacker with multiple rounds, from low to high since he couldn't use his gun sights. The first Black Talon hollow point round hit the man's middle section just above the belt line. The second and third rounds his only about two and four inches above that. The man was being thrown backwards from the impacts at that point and because of the new angle of his body the fourth round tore a trench up the length of his throat, entered through his chin and blew the top of his head off. The fifth round missed altogether.

Clive took in a deep breath and instantly knew he had a few cracked ribs from the shot he took. Not knowing if there were any other threats around, he willed himself to get up. Once he determined there was no one else coming for him Clive holstered his handgun, grabbed the dead man's revolver, retrieved his flashlight, and quickly headed back to his bike.

Still hopped up on adrenaline Clive decided to take advantage of mother nature's pain medicine and get home fast, rather than to continue focusing on safety and security. He decided to leave his backpack in the basket but threw a bungy cord over it to secure it. He gingerly got onto his bike and began to pedal harder than he'd ever pedaled in his life.

Forty-five grueling minutes later Clive was in the middle of the best group hug of his life with the three most important people in the world. He was wet, cold, and injured, but he was alive. He told them he was not going back to work. In between sobs he told them he loved them. Holly knew he'd been through something traumatic. Clive would tell her in his own time. He'd kept his promise.

About the Author — C.A. Moll

C.A. Moll is a proud father and grandfather from who has worked in the field of public safety for over 30 years. Born and raised on the west coast, he migrated from southern California to Washington State over 20 years ago. He brings a unique but realistic perspective of what a major disaster or nationwide collapse would look like due to decades of direct observation of human behavior and interactions during moments of crisis. He enjoys hiking, camping, reading, self-sufficiency projects, and prepping. He finds joy in family activities that are both fun and educational in the world of survival.

His first foray into the world of writing, he offers a spectacularly well told tale of the end.

CHAPTER 6 — FAMILY

I was having a lonely day today. It wasn't often that I felt this way since the final war. I had retreated to my grandfather's old prospecting camp in northern Ontario. Yes, I was one of the lucky ones that got away. It's been six years since that dreadful time. Six years since I have seen another human, red or white. But I do have a friend. It was the second year after the war, and I was out on my trap line. To my dismay, it was a fruitless trip that day. As I returned home, to my shock, I saw two small plastic Christmas trees. They were obviously old tree ornaments from when Christmas was still celebrated.

I slowly reached out to touch them and make sure my eyes weren't playing tricks on me. They hung from a large, old yellow birch tree, one of my favourite trees. They were in fact, real. The hairs on my arms stood on end. *Someone is near!* I thought to myself. I remember being afraid. I thought, *What if it was the reds, or even worse... the whites.*

I looked at the ornaments a little closer. There

was a note attached to the back of one. I hesitated; this was all a bit much to take in. Isolation increases sensitivity and I was on high alert. I opened the note and it read, "Find your Christmas tree and mark it with this."

I pondered as to the meaning. I could only assume that this stranger has chosen the yellow birch since the other ornament was tied tightly to a branch. I peered out to see if I could see anything but there was nothing around.

I went back home, and I was on edge. I had the ornament and note still clasped in my hand.

My home was cozy with a small wood stove, a bed, table and chair, and a cupboard. I remember tossing the ornament onto the table and there it stayed for a few days. *My Christmas tree....* I thought long and hard as to what my tree would be. My favourite tree is an old beech tree, but it was far away, and I wasn't sure if this stranger would find it. But then I thought distance might be safer, so I decided that the beech would be my choice and I would hang the ornament on it the next day.

And so, I did just that. I knew that keeping track of the days and time would prove to be beneficial for my survival. I knew when to harvest, when to plant, when to conserve. All of it was important to me. So, on December 24, I walked to the beech tree and was somewhat relieved that the ornament still hung there, but on the ground below it was a burlap sack. I looked around since I was again wary of this situation. There was no movement anywhere. It was softly snowing but it wasn't that cold.

I took the sack and opened it. Inside was a book,

a bottle of meat, and a candle. I looked at the objects in complete awe. Such wonderful things to get this day and age. The book was of music. The bottled meat was what I later discovered to be bear meat.

I returned home and set my gifts on the table. I was so impressed and was feeling cheery. I thought of what I could give in return. I had settled on a jar of moose meat. Jars were my saving grace. They were a pain to get them here but were worth their weight in gold to have. I also added a book of my sketches, a bottle of chokecherry wine... *my prize*, and one of my favourite wool blankets.

I hurried to the big old yellow birch and stashed the presents at the base. The small plastic Christmas tree was still swaying in the breeze. I was as giddy as a schoolboy. This stranger was changing my world in so many ways. I went back home and opened the music book, I opened my window, fetched my fiddle, and began to play. I took joy at the thought of my secret Santa enjoying my music somewhere close by.

That was all four years ago and we've been exchanging gifts every year since. I have never met my secret Santa, but I did wonder who it was. Was it a man or a woman? Young or old? It was a mystery, but I liked it.

This wasn't the only strange happening that had occurred. The strangest by far had happened last year. It was a heavy snow and food was scarce. I had finally run out of shells for my rifle and was at a loss as to how I would hunt.

I was aware of the pack of wolves that seemed to live by me, but they were shy, I guess — for which I'm very thankful. I had always left the remains of my kills in hopes of appeasing their hunger and maybe they wouldn't see me as their next meal.

It was a cold January when I was out splitting firewood. I thought I could hear something, so I stopped what I was doing. I could have sworn that I heard howling. Chills ran up my spine at the sound. They were off in the distance but still a little close for comfort.

I tried to ignore the woeful howls and continued to chop wood. I was suddenly startled by the quick arrival of two ravens who were cawing loudly from a jack pine next to my cabin. I put the axe down and stared at the birds in wonder. They took off and flew north to another jack pine and started cawing again. I could still hear the howling, as it was coming from the north as well.

I was puzzled as to what was going on. I went into the cabin, grabbed my scarf and toque, and went out again. I followed the ravens as they seemed to want me to do so. They flew from tree to tree as I stumbled along after them. I could see a small clearing ahead, and low and behold, I could see a male moose thrashing around on the ground. I had noticed that the howling had stopped, and the ravens perched at a distance and fell silent as well.

The bull was exhausted as I could see his back leg was slashed and blood was seeping into the snow all around.

I had no idea what was going on, but I knew that I was staring at at least a couple months' worth of food. I knew it was dangerous to get close but I only had my hunting knife and so I'd have to try to get in and cut the throat. He was a young bull and only had small antlers, but they were still lethal.

The bull would thrash, trying to get up but it was too wounded. It would then lay down, exhausted for a few moments. That was my chance. I threw myself on his body and struggled to get a hold of his antler to hold his head down. He was a powerful beast, but he was too tired to fight long. I had my knife out and slit his throat then I jumped back. The bull thrashed violently as he bled out. In a few quick moments he lay still and finally died.

I knew I had to be quick to clean him and started to work. I was in the middle when movement caught my eye. I was startled by two wolves who sat at the fringe of the clearing. They were staring at me with hungry eyes and I was alarmed. But instead of taking off, I slowly continued to separate the hind quarters of the moose. I kept looking up at the wolves who were still sitting there. I then noticed a small pup come from behind them, and it too, sat with its elders, licking its chops.

I could have taken more of the moose but decided that that would be pressing my luck. I took the hind quarters and carried them back towards my cabin. I stopped to look while the small pack moved in towards the kill. The wolves were cautious as they approached, keeping a steady eye on me. The ravens were cawing again, as they too, closed in on the kill. There were seven wolves and three pups. The pups were playing with each other as the elders gorged on what I had left. Even the ravens were playing with the pups as they waited for their turn at the feast.

I turned and headed back to my cabin, where I was hoping that I had enough jars for my take.

I hurried home as fast as I could, considering the weight of my share. I rushed inside and filled my canning pot on the stove. I would be busy for a while as I bottled the moose meat and stored them away in my cupboard.

I was amazed that the wolves seemed to be working with me, like I was a part of their pack. The ravens would visit me from time to time and I'd give them bits of meat as a treat. I felt as if I was one with nature, a feeling I never had before. I was raised to be afraid of the wolves... yet here they were, helping me survive, as I helped them. In my experience, not even people were this civil — with the exception of my secret Santa.

I don't know why the stranger did not seem to want to meet in person, but I respected that. I often wondered if we would ever meet, but I only knew them through our Christmas exchanges.

It was Christmas of this year that my heart had sunk. My secret Santa had not left their gifts at my beech tree, nor did they retrieve my gifts at the yellow birch. I waited days, which turned into weeks, but there was no sign. I had given them a bottle of moose meat, another book of my sketches, and a silver serving spoon. But the stranger did not come.

I was disheartened. Never had I ever felt so alone. I worried for the stranger's safety. I didn't even play my fiddle because I was so forlorn. Although it did make my visits from the ravens that much more special. I was so alone.

A few times I thought to go look for this stranger but decided against it each time. It was too dangerous to venture far from the cabin. I wasn't worried about the wolves, but I was afraid of the bears, or of me getting lost. Sometimes you can follow your snow tracks back, but the wind can rise quickly and cover them. Besides, I wouldn't even know where to start looking. I have travelled around my area and didn't see anything that could be a habitation.

I thought of the stranger often. I feared the worst, that my friend had succumbed to some horrible fate. Those dark thoughts did not help my mood. It was then that I first considered the rope and the rafter. It was a dark time for me.

One day, in February, I was again splitting some firewood when my raven friends appeared. They were acting different this time. Instead of asking for some nibbles, they cawed at me and flew to the southwest, where they perched and called again to me. I knew they wanted me to follow them, so I went and put my scarf on and hurriedly followed them.

The snow was deep, and walking was difficult. The ravens carried on to the southwest with me in tow.

I had been walking for about two hours when my heart stopped. In the distance was a small cabin with a steady stream of smoke rising from the chimney. I quickly ducked behind a tree. The ravens perched on the same tree I was hiding behind and were cawing incessantly. I tried to shush, them but if anything, they got louder. I could see the door of the cabin open and I found that I was holding my breath. I peeked again and saw a figure hobble outside. They had a splint on their leg which caused the leg to remain straight. The person was a woman with stark black hair and high cheekbones. She was beautiful and I couldn't stop looking.

She looked over to where I and the noisy ravens were. She looked alarmed. I took a deep breath and stepped out into the open. She was startled to see me but still remained calm.

"Come closer!" she hollered. The words sounded alien to me since it's been so long since I heard another's voice.

I ventured a little closer although my hairs were standing on end. All kinds of thoughts were racing around in my mind. The stories that I heard about cannibals after the war were at the forefront. They would set traps and dine on the unwary. But against my fear, I slowly walked over to the woman. She was obviously as nervous as I was, which made me feel a little better.

"Who are you?" she asked in a shaky voice.

My mind was blank, I haven't had the need to say my name for ages. "Jim...." I responded.

She was still calm but alert. "Beech tree?"

A wave of relief came over me. "Yes, the beech tree!" I exclaimed. Then I said, "Yellow birch?"

She smiled, "Yes, the yellow birch." she said. We both stood in awe of each other. Did I mention that she was beautiful? Well she was. She looked part Cree to me, but I could've been wrong. "My secret Santa. I'm Cheryl" she cooed.

I smiled, "That's what I called you too!" I said in surprise.

She looked as relieved as I was, "Sorry I didn't get there this year." she said. "But as you can see...." she gestured towards her leg in the splint.

I was concerned, "What happened?" I asked.

She laughed softly, "I'm pretty clumsy and

tripped down a crevice. It took me a long time to get back here with a broken leg and all. It was not fun!" she said, shaking her head. She refocused on me, "I knew you were kind, but I was so afraid anyways. I couldn't take the risk."

"I was afraid too. I heard too many horror stories about after the war." I said.

"You and me both!" she exclaimed.

She had invited me in her humble abode, and we sat and talked through the night. She had been a schoolteacher in the old world. I told her that I was a conductor on the train when the world went to hell.

She had a wonderful sense of humour and her laugh was angelic. The next morning, after a quick nap, the ravens had returned and were cawing. I stepped outside and could tell that they wanted me to follow again, hopefully to my cabin. I coaxed her to come with me since my cabin was far better equipped compared to her little shanty.

It took us a long time to return to my cabin, but the ravens were patient for us. I lit the stove and again we talked for some time. She was so intelligent and a delight to converse with. It was a milder day, so we went out on the porch with some rosehip tea. She was sore from the trek and I was winded as well.

That was when the real magic happened. I brought out my fiddle and began to play. While doing so, the ravens returned and perched on the jack pine. They seemed keen to listen. Suddenly, I noticed the wolves were sitting off in the distance. Their heads were cocked to the left then the right as they seemed to be fascinated by the music.

I played like I had never played before. Cheryl's

feet were stomping and even the wolves howled in sync. The ravens came and settled on the bannister and were cawing.

It was an amazing day. I felt like I had my own family for the first time in my life. I continued to play long into the night as Cheryl minded the candles and the fire.

I was truly blessed on this cool February night. I was truly blessed, indeed.

About the Author — G. Neil Trochymchuk

Neil has been writing since he was young. He enjoys reading and being outdoors. His favourite genre is horror, sci-fi, and fantasy.

CHAPTER 7 — SHIPWRECKED SANTA

Eddie Hampton's backpack thudded against his frame, heavy with the cans of Spam and sardines he had raided from the galley as he sloshed through the ankle-deep water in the ship's inner halls. He had been in a lot of tight spots since the world had ended... but running down a dark hallway from a couple of seafaring zombies on Christmas Eve with no clear escape was probably the tightest of all the spots. The ship was going to sink and there wasn't a damn thing he could do about it with a couple of hungry, water-bloated zombies hot on his heels.

He stopped at the T in the hall, just long enough to catch his breath, bringing the good-'ol rebar up to his chest and holding it at the ready in case he'd gained less ground than he thought—or in case there were another one or two of them lurking in the shadows ahead. *Eddie! Damn you! You were an idiot to think this was going to be an easy trip!* He thought to himself, throwing in a couple more curse words for good measure as he panted quietly, listening to the low, wet gurgles, and rushing water sounds that echoed through the stinking maze of darkness.

He closed his eyes to calm himself, then nearly laughed at the idea that closing his eyes in a dark, zombie-filled hallway on a sinking ship would make him feel calmer. Instead, he decided to just remind himself why he wouldn't lay down and get eaten by some gross, hungry zombies — or drown.... He wasn't doing this for himself and that made him a hero — a good guy. Good guys don't die in the middle of the story.

The thought made him feel better for a minute, then his headlight flickered, threatening to extinguish his only source of light. *If that happens....* Eddie shut the thought down. He couldn't let himself think it if he planned on surviving.

If Eddie was a survivor, then he had to keep his focus on getting out of here alive and it had to happen pretty much right now, because the water was lapping at his knees already as the ship made its nosedive for the ocean floor. That's what somebody who was gonna survive would do, so that's what he was gonna do.

Eddie used to be the kind of guy that wouldn't make it out — a real loser, but he was different now. He was Apocalypse Eddie and Apocalypse Eddie was a damn hero!

That's why he was in this predicament, wasn't it?

Earlier that week he'd noticed that the ship seemed a lot further out than it was before. He told the kids it was probably just a bit of motion from last week's storm, but Suzie had a different theory about what was happening. It was something about what happened in the bay... what was it called? Upwelling? Anyway, it happened in the winter around here and it would push the surface water out to sea, dragging the ship with it.

A loud clatter signaled that one of the dead things had fallen over something. *Come on, you rotten bag of flesh. Time to meet your end!* He wanted to say it out loud, but he didn't dare. He hadn't made it this far into the end of humanity by making dumb mistakes. He knew he needed to keep his mouth shut until he was ready to make his move. Then he had to kill them fast and make a break for it.

Alright Eddie, he thought, readying himself for the task, *no time like the present to make a daring, life-threatening break for the surface with a bag full of Christmas Spam, right?*

He could smell the approaching zombies now. The stench of bloated, rotting flesh made him want to vomit, but he knew he could manage, just like he always did. The thick rebar waited in his left hand, ready to do its damage as soon as the first creature came around the corner. His light flickered another whisper of warning that he was running out of time. *You better stay on, you piece of....*

He whirled around the corner at the same moment the first creature appeared, sticking the rebar straight into the zombie's eye-socket. The thing sunk to the floor, the real dead kind of dead. As Eddie pulled against the sucking pressure to retrieve his weapon, the second creature appeared.

Without taking time to recover, Eddie swung the metal with all his might, much like he used to swing his old baseball bat before his coach had taught him how to do it right. The heavy piece hit the thing square in its rotting skull. There was a sick squelching sound as the rebar sunk in. He could tell just by the feel of it that the hit hadn't been enough. He'd have to do it over again to really get the thing down. With a twist of his wrist he had the weapon ready again. His eyes focused on the light, taking in the hunching thing with half its face sunken in and blackish blood dripping over swollen lips.

The second blow did the job. The thing splashed into the water without further sound or protest. Before he could stop himself, Eddie let out a victorious whoop. The sound echoed off the metal walls of the hull, alerting the others. A chorus of hisses and growls cried out in response, making him instantly regret his mistake. Eddie tightened the heavy pack on his shoulders, ready as he would ever be to make his exit.

"You ain't stopping me now assholes. It's Christmas and I've got kids to get home to!" He bellowed at them through the dark maze as his light flickered.

Eddie plunged himself forward, moving through the rising water with a deliberate stride. The sloshing sound made it difficult to listen, but he didn't really see any other way to get through it. Another zombie shambled around the corner, splashing and grunting loudly.

"Hey Captain!" Eddie called out to it, feeling like a madman as he plundered forward to make contact.

What had once been the ship's captain lunged for him, falling forward into the water. Eddie plunged the rebar down into the base of its skull, ignoring the sound of another kill. *You get used to it,* he thought as three more creatures appeared ahead of him, cutting off his escape.

"Ah, crap!" He breathed out into the stinking air. *Time for plan B.*

Eddie really didn't want to come up with a plan B, but every good survivalist had one—that was one of George's sayings. The kid had adopted it from one of those cheesy survivalist guides meant for kids that Eddie had brought him from the burnt-down bookstore. The pages were a little crisp, but overall, the book was in alright shape.

He flung himself into one of the dark rooms, pushing the door through resistant currents of water until the latch slid into place and locked him in. He looked around in the strobe of light, hoping there was a big enough window for his plan B. The room had a little window—maybe two feet across. Eddie studied it, trying to decide if he had a hope of fitting through.

"Thank god for the apocalypse weight loss plan." Eddie murmured to himself as he approached the dual-paned glass.

He dropped the pack from his shoulder and held it up to the opening to see if it would fit. *Maybe.* He laughed, causing the creatures on the other side of the door to wail with frustration. Their cries reminded him that there's no going back once you decide to switch plans.

"Alright, Eddie. You're going to get yourself and this food out of here and get home in time for Christmas dinner!" He told himself, setting the pack down and pulling the Model 23 Glock from its holster and taking aim at the barrier between him and the open ocean — or bay, at least. He'd heard somewhere that the Glock could fire under water. He hoped it was true… because he was about to go for a swim.

"I'm gonna put all this Spam under the damn Christmas tree!" He shouted, before pulling the trigger.

The sound roared through his skull. At the same instant, the glass shattered. It imploded and exploded with the battling pressure of the blast and the hundreds of pounds of ocean water. Eddie shook his head, attempting but failing, to clear out the ringing. He holstered the gun and brought up the rebar so that he could chip away at any of the jagged pieces of glass. There weren't many. The pressure of the incoming water blasted the rigid opening into a smooth portal.

Eddie waited for the room to fill, trying to take calming, even breaths, but really just panting at the thought of the sheer amount of water between him and the surface. When the water was level with the bottom of the window, he forced the pack through, holding it so that it sat suspended just outside the window, waiting for him. When the water was level with the top, he sucked in the largest breath he could manage and went for it, arms first.

His shoulders passed through without much issue, then, with a little bit of wiggling, he managed the gun and his hips, but when the time came for his feet to pass through, the knee-high waders that had kept him mostly dry and warm caught against the edge. In a moment of panic, he yanked his foot forward. It came free, leaving the boot behind.

Eddie forced his eyes open. Above him, the pale light of the moon reflected off the surface, blotted out in places by towering tendrils of kelp. He started kicking, free from the metal hell that would have been his grave, eyes fixed on the light. But the light kept shrinking. Though he kicked with all his might, he was only getting dragged further down by the weight of the stuffed pack.

Eddie worked his whole body, thrashing and thrusting so frantically that he lost the other boot and still he made no progress. His head spun with the effort, making his lungs feel as though they might burst. Eddie fought against the rising panic as he sunk further away from the silvery ripples of the surface. He could feel the end of his breath. If he didn't let go his body would revolt and he would expel the spent air, forcing water in until he was drowned…

His head burst through the surface with the subtlety of a breaching whale. He gasped and sputtered, his lungs screaming for air. He stayed like that, thinking of nothing but breathing… until the burning feeling was gone and the ache of cold water on his tired body took over.

"Fifty degrees, Eddie. It's fifty degrees. You're not gonna freeze," he told himself as he turned over on the surface, looking for rescue.

He found it about twenty-five yards further out than he had left it, with the anchor tangled in the kelp beds. *Lucky for that, or I'd be swimming to shore.* Eddie threw his arms over the side of the dinghy, resting there for a quick moment before tossing the rebar over. It landed with a hollow clatter against the composite surface as Eddie ran his hands along the edge of the craft, looking for the rope ladder.

The dang thing seemed to be hung up on

something. He tugged at it again, trying to adjust his grip on the side of the dinghy for more leverage. With a final tug the ladder came loose, pulling another water-logged zombie with it. Eddie hadn't specifically been expecting the zombie, but he'd learned to handle a lot of unexpected things in the last year, so his reaction was enough to keep the thing from biting him straight out.

Eddie kicked it with his socked feet, feeling the body give as it struggled in the water. Reflexively he grabbed for his rebar, but then remembered he'd already offered it up to the boat. Instead he grabbed for his gun, sliding it out of the holster and flipping it around in one smooth motion, not ready to test the firing under water theory. He brought up the weapon and bashed his attacker in the side of the head, stunning it long enough to pull free.

Eddie hoisted his tired body into the boat, relieved but not able to rest yet. He grabbed the rebar, turning around to see the zombie pulling at the ladder as if to make its way back into the boat. The rebar pierced through the rotting skull with a downward thrust. Eddie used the rebar like a skewer to move the dead thing away from the dinghy before shaking it off so that it bobbed, bloated and gas-filled above the kelp.

You get used to it. He thought again, but this time with less certainty than before. *It's what a hero has to do,* he told himself, starting up the motor and pointing the craft back toward the docks. Doubt crept in as he steered through the milky fog. Was he a hero? He'd lost the food. A hero doesn't panic and drop the supplies to save himself.

Eddie had become a lot of things since the world

collapsed. But what was he actually if he wasn't a hero? Each time he killed one of the creatures he painted himself as the good guy — Apocalypse Eddie and promised himself that every day of survival brought him further away from the person he was before.

The wind whipped at Eddie's overgrown, soaking hair as he moved back toward land, making him feel cold and miserable as he thought about what he was. He knew what his next move would have to be — if he were going to give the kids a real Christmas this year like he'd promised. He would have to go back to the office — the place where it all began — and pick up the ratty old Santa suit. That would be a good start. He could be Santa Claus, even if Santa showed up without his boots. He looked down at his drenched wool socks and smirked. The kids would really get a chuckle about that.

Safe on land again Eddie moved silently through the night. His wet socks padding on cracked asphalt as he listened to the dark, keen to avoid any land encounters with the creeping dead. As he made his way toward the old building, Eddie thought about the last time he wore the suit to play Santa at the office party. He'd let his beard hang down around his neck, too lazy, and too drunk to really play the part. That's when Shelly Parker sauntered up to him. He remembered the way she sat on his lap, wearing that skirt that was way too short for a work party. His heart thudded and his blood rushed as he let his hands run down her legs and she leaned in to whisper in his ear. Then he took her up on the offer, only to get busted in the act by her husband when he burst into her office.

Eddie shook his head. *No.* He was a different

person. He was a good guy now, not a rotten, home-wrecking prick. He had kids to take care of. He'd lost about twenty pounds and quit smoking and drinking. He had purpose. Everything changed when it all went down.

Wind tore through the quiet little bay town as he hurried, cursing at the way the cold tore through his wet clothes and trying to decide if it was worth an extra stop. He could jump through the broken window of the souvenir shop to see if there were any more scarves left in the rubble. Maybe he could grab a couple cheesier presents for George and Suzie while he was at it.

The thought of his kids, waiting at home in the dark for him to return changed his mind. The whole point of this trip was to give them the opposite of what had happened last year. It was time to get home.

Eddie passed the old taqueria next to the office. The busted-out door flapped open then closed in the wind. He walked past it, remembering the day he'd braved the streets for the first time. He was so hungry. All he really wanted was a frozen burrito—the kind that Stan used to keep in the break room freezer. Eddie used to steal them all the time, then laugh at Stan's whole-office inquiry emails. *Yeah, you were a real winner, weren't you Eddie?* He shook his head, dipping through the broken glass under the metal bar of the office door.

His feet crunched on the rocky glass shards as he made his way deeper into the office, remembering burrito day. He knew that the office had a backup generator, so maybe, just maybe, the freezer hadn't been out all that long... and if there were any burritos, they wouldn't be rotten.

They were rotten, of course, and that was the first day he'd ever killed anyone. Shelly Parker. There he was bitching about rotten burritos in the freezer when she'd shambled toward him, gurgling in a bloodstained blouse with all the buttons torn out, as if he were one of those stupid burritos.

Back then he wasn't ready for it. Sure, he'd seen them on the streets, but he thought they'd all moved on or died off. He'd been holed up in his little apartment living off a forty-pound bag of rice and sriracha sauce. The navy or the army or somebody like that had already come through and shot all those things to hell. That was what the news said before the channels all went dark. So why would he have thought that there were any left?

But Shelly was there, and she was gonna kill him for sure. She had that hungry, dead look that they all have, but that was the first he'd seen it up close. He wrestled with her, the whole time screaming, "Shelly! It's me, Ed! Shelly! C'mon, what the hell!" While she lurched at him, nearly biting his face off over and over again as he panicked.

He grabbed the only thing he could find. Edna's silver serving spoon, still left out from the holiday party, and jammed it through her eye socket. It hadn't been a planned move at all. It was luck more than anything clever on Eddie's part. In fact, Eddie remembered as he stepped over the dust of another body, retracing his steps, the whole reason he'd made it that long was nothing but luck.

Eddie was a loner and a loser before all of this. He was sitting at home eating take-out pizza and watching bad Christmas movie re-runs while the rest of the world spent time together... spreading whatever the dang disease was. When the CDC warning came out, Eddie had already been alone, inside for nearly five days straight. That's the only reason he didn't get infected while the rest of the world fell apart. It was just luck.

Eddie had stabbed Shelly straight through the eye. She sunk down with a sound that came out like a mix of a sigh and a moan. When it was done, he'd puked all over the break room floor. He didn't know if it was murder to kill Shelly like that. One of the last broadcasts before everything went dark was some sort of ethical talk about it on News 10. Eddie had fallen asleep on the couch before he heard the conclusion, but right then he would have given anything to know.

Shelly. Eddie had always had a major crush on her, even though she'd been married to the top sales guy, Chris Parker. Chris was an asshole. Eddie had barely felt bad about getting caught in her office that night. At least until she started sobbing and Chris walked out on her. Shelly had turned to Eddie for comfort and he'd shrugged her off. What was he supposed to do about it? She was the one cheating.

Eddie passed the open door to the breakroom, where he'd stood over her bloody, dead body. He thought about her very alive body in the office the night of the party, with the smell of spilled vodka soaking into a stack of papers on her desk next to the picture of her kids.

Her kids. That's what had gotten him moving that day as if he were waking up from a daze. He realized that Shelly Parker had been locked in the office this whole time, having turned, or died, or whatever the disease did… before he took her brains out with a silver serving spoon. There Eddie was, puking and feeling sorry for himself, when he realized that Shelly had a couple of kids out there somewhere.

He stooped down to pick the suit up off of the floor, feeling the flimsy fabric. He righted himself to look at the picture of the two kids smiling up at the camera as time folded in on him again. Yeah, that was the day that everything changed for him. He turned from a loser, a no-good homewrecker without anybody to care for, into the good guy. He'd grabbed the broom from the break room closet and made his way back to this very spot, killing two more of the zombie things that used to be his coworkers on the way. He'd found her purse and her home address and decided to check on the kids.

The Santa suit hung on Eddie's lean frame as he made his way out of that place. Back on the street he felt better — like Apocalypse Eddie again. As he made his way past the business district, an idea occurred to him. Didn't old Mrs. Anderson used to have an orange tree in the front yard? Yeah, that's right. He'd always tuck his head down when he walked to work to avoid engaging her or he'd end up carrying a sticky brown sack of 'em into the office.

He licked his lips, thinking about what a fool he'd been to turn down such an offer. Sad, loner Eddie didn't want to talk to old ladies or share sticky oranges with Chris Parker and the other jerks in the office. But Santa Eddie? Yeah, he wanted to fill the whole sack with sweet fruit.

"Ho! Ho! Ho! Santa's got a plan." He breathed

out into the mist, making a sharp turn toward Mrs. Anderson's orange tree. The tree cast a dark shadow against the milky night, seeming to move in the stillness. Eddie squinted, feeling pretty certain that a tree shouldn't sway without wind. That's when he noticed more than the tree. In the dark of the night a mother black bear pushed up against the branches, snapping them down for her yearling cubs.

"Aren't you assholes supposed to be hibernating!?" He moaned.

But Eddie knew that wasn't the case for the bears that came down from the hills around here—again, something about the upwelling, Suzie had told him.

If they're here for the upwelling, they should be at the shore. Eddie thought to himself, reaching under Santa's suit for the Glock. It was time to find out if it was waterproof. He could bring the oranges tonight and come back for the meat tomorrow morning.

Eddie had no idea how to field dress a bear. The apocalypse survival curve was steep, and he hadn't made it all the way to the top yet. There were too many cans, and boxes, and bags of food that never went bad. Sure, he knew that the time would come when he'd have to suck it up and hunt, but it hadn't come yet.

Eddie relaxed his grip, bending his elbows as he watched the trio pillage his orange tree and ruin his plan. He'd have to kill the mother bear first or she'd probably tear him in half. Maybe the sound of the gun would scare off the cubs so that he wouldn't have to shoot them. He didn't need three bears-worth of meat. He wasn't greedy. Really, he'd be fine with just the oranges.

The mother bear paused, as though she could sniff Eddie's intent on the air. He bolstered himself in case she decided to charge. But instead of charging she turned to the smaller of the two cubs, nudging it back toward the pile of fruit on the ground before resuming her own feast. Eddie knew she could sense his presence. She just didn't care. He wasn't a threat to her.

He stood there thinking as he watched the lumbering beasts munch away, the juice of his oranges soaking into their matted fur. Even if they ran, the cubs probably wouldn't survive the winter without their mother. *What sort of a guy does that to a couple of kids?* He couldn't escape the thought. And what if he missed? If she didn't kill him, she'd probably get a few good hits in. What good would he be to his kids if that happened?

A time would come when Eddie would have no choice but to hunt, but it didn't have to be today. Not for a bag of fruit, anyway. And, besides, when the time was right, he would start with something small, like a squirrel. That's what George's book would tell him to do.

He returned the Glock to its holster and backed away from the orange tree without making a sound. The bears would move on by morning and they could all come and pick the leftover oranges together. Nobody had to die tonight—not for a sack of sweets.

Eddie made his way down the street empty-handed. His mission was a complete failure. He'd gone out to score enough food to last them through the rest of the wet season and had come back with nothing but a threadbare Santa suit and bare feet. Despite his failures, he found himself whistling an amalgamation of every Christmas song he could remember. Sure, maybe it was the lack of his heavy boots, but he could swear this was the lightest he'd felt in a long time walking up to the door. So, he wasn't the hero of the apocalypse, but he'd made it back alive again. He didn't have a sack full of Christmas secrets. The kids would spend Christmas with an empty-handed, bootless Santa, but at least they wouldn't be alone this year. He didn't know what that made him, but whatever it was, it was good enough.

About the Author — Jill Davies

Jill Davies is a scientist by trade and education, but she's given up the hard stuff to write science fiction. She spent her early years working in laboratories without windows, running CSI-worthy equipment and imagining up fantastical worlds set in distant futures. It took her ten more years and another career as a high school science teacher before she decided to commit to being a full-time mom and writer.

When she's not changing diapers or typing furiously at her computer she likes to disappear into the trails, running late into the night and talking about her stories to anyone who will listen. Her first book-- Due North, is set to be released this winter. You can find out more about it at jillndavies.com, or dive deeper into her strange world. If you'd like regular updates on what she's up to, you can sign up for her mailing list, or read her blog.

CHAPTER 8 — A GOOD SIGN

"Well, Bear, what'll it be?" asked Kris to his canine companion.

Kris and Bear stood at a gravel fork in the road, a street sign mocking their path. The wooden post had long been shattered, and the street names no longer mattered. The sign, now twisted metal and shorn with bullet holes, was half buried in snow. Bear looked up at the old man and wagged his tail slowly.

"I ain't got nothing for you. Not till later."

Bear sat.

Kris knelt.

The old man raised a weathered hand to bury his fingers in the warmth of Bear's fur which shielded a bony frame beneath. Bear remained stoic, looking ahead. Listening. There were no birds, no crickets. Just a snow-covered path to the left or to the right. Neither held the promise of success or failure. Just an option.

"We could go left. Looks like there's some tree cover that way off in the distance, maybe."

Bear licked himself.

"We could go right. Might be some water or field grouse that way."

They watched as nothing moved up ahead. Kris looked up to the horizon, raising a hand to the setting sun. He stacked another hand on it, measuring the sun's distance to the horizon with his fingers. Seven. Seven fingers from the top of the horizon to the bottom of the sun.

"A little over an hour and a half before sunset," he said, lowering his hands. "Better head left and see if we can reach some tree cover by nightfall."

He leaned on his side to stand, supporting himself with a knee and an outstretched arm. His pack shifted on his shoulders, pulling at him to stay put. A groan came from somewhere as he stood upright. He brushed the snowpack from his fingerless gloves and his knees. Bear made a slow circle, before following at his heel. The heavy black boots on Kris' feet sank in the unstable snow as they walked. Their footsteps were the first to tread here. Untouched snow crunched beneath them. No plows. No tire tracks. No footprints. Except theirs. Snowdrifts, like giant white teeth gnashing at the roadside clamored at the side of the road, frozen in place where the wind had finally stopped not long ago.

"Got a surprise for you, Bear. I've been setting it aside for some time now. Just for the occasion."

Kris tapped a side pocket on his pack and felt for the can to make sure it was still there, a habit formed over the past few weeks. Daily affirmation. Sometimes several times a day. At daybreak, before dusk, every time they stop. He checked to make sure it was still there, this simple little thing that he'd been setting aside... ever since he found it in a cabinet somewhere along the way.

As they walked, their shadows grew longer, legs long and lean against the path. Their bodies were alien invaders. Kris adjusted his headscarf and covered more of his gray beard. The wind began to pick up and wisps of snow started covering their path. It whipped at his headscarf.

Bear stopped.

Kris stopped. He looked up ahead, watching the dog with a sidelong glance. Kris reached for his boot and unclipped a buttoned-down leather strap to reveal a throwing knife, pulling it out slowly. Bear took a step toward the ditch bank along the side of the road, lowering his head and sniffing. Another step. Kris wound up, ready to launch, intent, focused. Another step. Kris watched. Another step.

Then came a clamor in the ditch bank, followed by a bird, launching into the air, flapping, and fighting the wind as Bear advanced with striking speed. But he missed, chomping at the air. The unmistakable long, decorative tail of a white ring-neck pheasant struggled against the high winds, managing to get higher than Bear's jaws in mid-flight. Kris flung the knife, and it hit its mark with a thud. The pheasant rolled from the sky and plummeted to the ground. Bear captured the kill, giving it a shake before returning to the road where he dropped it at Kris' feet.

"Atta boy, Bear! What a feast!"

Kris rustled the dog's fur and inspected the kill. His knife was gone. Kris looked up at the trail of red dots on the snow. He followed the path, looking for any sign of the blade. The snow began to glow orange as clouds formed in the distance, blotting portions of the skyline with peach and purple. He saw a tiny hole in the snow and plunged his hand inside, stirring the depth with his fingers. After a few seconds, he pulled his hand out, shaking it off and blowing warm air on his exposed fingertips. They were now red with cold, but he tried again. After a few seconds, he pulled out the blade. Snow stuck to the sides but melted at his fingers. He wiped the blade clean, returning it to the sheath and tucked his hand into the warmth of his armpit. Bear wagged his tail as he saw Kris coming back.

"Well done, buddy. Well done."

He returned to the gravel road where Bear stood by the kill. Kris reached for it and Bear licked the melting snow from his hand.

"That's enough now. We better get moving."

They walked until they reached a small cluster of overgrown shrubs and a few tall evergreen trees in a slender valley off the gravel road. At a fair distance, they watched, waiting for a sign of movement. A rustle of any kind. A sound. Nothing. Kris crouched down and pulled a small monocular from his bag, holding it to his eye. Through the lens, a tangled mess of dead and dormant branches crosshatched the patch of brush. A single track of deer footprints trailed off to one side. A few tall evergreens peaked from the middle. He lowered the sight piece and looked to Bear, who was blowing puffs of steam from his mouth with each breath. No perked ears, no standing hair on the nape, no rigid tail. A good sign.

Kris returns the lens to his pack in the same pouch it came from. The last red glow of daylight begins to illuminate the tops of the trees.

APOCALYPTIC WINTER — BOOK TWO

"Looks like we made the right choice," Kris says, partially to himself.

Three days ago, he marked the solstice. The dawn came late. The day was short. The sun fell early. The night was long. And cold. As they approached the small wooded patch, Bear began to sniff around, marking the perimeter in typical canine fashion. Kris collected branches as he walked, snapping them to test for quality. He approached a dead tree and knelt next to it, pulling his bag from his shoulder. From inside, he removed and unraveled a small section of wire which was carefully coiled into a circle, and began working the wire at the base of the tree.

Eventually, the tree fell, and Kris continues with his wire saw, cutting rounds to length and stripping the limbs from it along the way. Bear peed nearby and looked back at him. Eventually, he lowered his leg and paced back to the old man. He sniffed at the limp pheasant on his pack.

"Hey!" he called out, shooing Bear with a soft backhand. "Get your snout out of there. We're saving that for Christmas dinner."

Bear sat.

The dog watched patiently as Kris dressed and buried the pheasant in a bed of snow.

"No," he says, pointing at the pheasant's shallow snow grave.

Kris loaded up his arms with wood and walked to a flat spot beneath a grove that snow hadn't yet touched. The low-lying branches of an evergreen managed to keep the weather at bay around the base. Pine needles and moss covered the skirt like a welcome mat to the estranged. A teepee in a tree.

He set the wood down in a pile and started a small fire near the edge of the dripline. As it grew, he added larger sticks and twigs, setting rocks around the base. The soft glow of firelight took over for the sun, which passed in silence not long ago. For a moment, he let the warmth take over until he could feel his hands again. Bear lay down next to him. A good sign.

Kris strung out some cordage and pulled a folded sheet of black plastic from his pack. Bear looked up for a moment, then rested his head again by the fire.

"Lazy bum," Kris said, securing the tarp and forming a sort of wind shield, rainfly, and light barrier with it beneath the branches. He braced it with a few limbs, careful not to puncture the plastic.

He pulled an aluminum canteen from the outside of his pack and removed the bottom sleeve, a container of sorts, scooping up a pile of snow. He set the tin by the fire and let the snow melt. As it started to boil, he added small snowballs, one by one, until the container was full. He counted as it boiled, somewhere near 600. Then he pulled back the container and filled his canteen with the boiled water and started all over again. But this time, he added a few pine needles to the water as it boiled.

"You know, my mom used to make this for me in the summertime, back when I was a kid," Kris said, half talking to Bear, half talking to no one in particular. "She said the secret to a good tea was a few pine needles."

Bear exhaled.

"I take it you already knew that."

The glow of the firelight started to grow and Kris stirred the embers. When he looked up, he noticed a small sapling across from the fire pit. It only had a few branches and several long pine needles on it.

"The new growth needles are the best," he continued.

Kris grabbed a stick and gave Bear a gentle poke. Bear's eyes moved, unimpressed. He pulled the container and swirled his tea, blowing the steam from the top before taking a sip. A wince and a swallow followed.

"Not bad," he said, putting the container down. "Hungry, Bear?"

Bear perked up with new life, waiting to see if the old man was serious. Kris rummaged through the side pocket in his pack and Bear got up to inspect. His tail wagged slightly. Kris pulled a small can from the pack and immediately concealed it with his hand. Bear pawed at the ground. He sat, wagging his tail, and waiting impatiently.

"You know what this is, don't you?"

Bear shifted his stance, licking his whiskers.

Kris uncovered the small tin can in his hand, revealing a stamped-on expiration date:
BEST IF USED BY
DEC 25 2025.

"We made it this far, my buddy Bear. And one day to spare."

Bear licked his whiskers again and a line of drool began to form on one side. Kris hesitated for a moment, feeling the weight of the can, the weight that he'll be missing from his pack. The knowledge of nothing left... then lifted the pull tab on the can, reading the label on the side as he does it. It has faded and become worn, but still showed signs of the original printing from a few years back. "Vienna Sausage." Inside, the characteristic formation of seven small sausages was arranged like a fag submerged beneath a gelatin coating. Bear inched closer. Kris stabbed one with a knife, giving it a twist and freeing it from the bunch. He pulled it out and broke off a piece for Bear. "Hey now, watch the fingers!" He did it again. Before he could remove another piece, the first piece was already down the hatch. "Jesus, did you even taste it?" he asked, handing over another piece.

Bear inhaled it again, the suction from his jowls matching his hunger. Kris arranged two of the small sausages onto a forked stick and held them near the fire. They sizzled and popped, and Bear sniffed at the aroma. After a few moments, Kris pulled them off and Bear watched him as he ate slowly, taking in the salt and flavor he'd long forgotten. The fire crackled as he ate.

In the distance, the silence was broken by the faint paka-paka of gunfire. There was a pause, then another shot. Bear looked to the east. Kris looked to the east, then back to his small tin can. He removed a full sausage and handed it to Bear, breaking the dog's concentration. But only for a moment.

"It's alright, Bear. Couple miles at least." Kris patted the dog's shoulder, looking toward the sound. "We'll be fine for now."

Kris finished the last of the sausages and offered his fingertips to Bear, who licked until he left nothing behind. Kris wiped his hand and got up to set the can beneath the sapling across the way. Then he piled rocks on the fire until the flames died out, smoldering to all but a faint orange glow. Kris reached for his pack once again to remove his bedding. He spread it beneath the makeshift shelter, creating a humble manger of sorts.

"You know, Bear," he started, "Legend has it that animals can speak on Christmas Eve."

Kris began to stretch out a blanket and Bear walked over, laying down on the bedding and curling his nose toward his tail.

"Don't be a bed-hog now," Kris said. "Say you can talk, I bet you'd say, 'My owner, he's the best. Saved me from that house fire and gave me Vienna Sausage on Christmas Eve.'"

Bear closed his eyes.

Kris stood, watching the dog at peace. His belly wasn't full, but it wasn't empty either. As Bear slipped into a dream state, he whimpered slightly, and his feet twitched with movement. Kris watched the fire die out and the light fade to dark. The waxing moon cast a fluorescent glow and night shadowed around him. He retrieved the rocks from the fire, now hot to the touch, and placed them near his bedroll beneath the pine needles and moss. He lay beside Bear and pulled up a cover. *It would appear that some angels prefer sleep over speech*, he thought to himself.

Kris awoke with the warm, wet shock of Bear's tongue across his forehead and winced at the shock. Bear continued.

"All right, I'm up. I'm up."

He looked around and remembered what he could of the night before. Everything looked different, as it usually does on the move. But just outside his evergreen cover was a blackened fire pit and a small sapling with an empty tin can at the base. Kris stood up and stretched, then relieved himself on a tree.

Bear did the same.

"Merry Christmas, Bear," he said. "What do you say we stay here and rest one more night? Have us a feast?"

Bear wagged his tail and wandered off to sniff around some bushes nearby. Kris uncovered the pheasant and brushed off the snow and ice. Then, he dug a small pit and layered it with leaves and brush. A bed for the dead. He removed the feet and the head, placing them aside, and put the bird on the leaves. Then he covered it with more leaves and brush. He added a few inches dirt and rock and brushed his hands in satisfaction.

Kris started a fire on top of the burial site and got more snow ready to boil. "Low and slow," Kris said. "Couple hours and we're good to go, Bear."

Bear looked back at the sound of his name, then returned to sniffing about. "You're welcome."

Kris tended to the fire, keeping it small but hot, so wet wood wouldn't give him away. He worked to reinforce his shelter, as the limbs had started to sag from the weight of new snow, and stockpiled dry wood under the tree. He ignored his hunger, working through it as the prospect of a mid-day feast drew near.

Bear returned to the shelter and curled up on the blanket, shifting now and then. Kris collected the small tin from beneath the sapling and joined him. Together, they sat and watched the fire as Kris tinkered with the can.

He cut the paper wrap from the can, carefully peeling it back and setting it aside. Then, he removed the lid and made a few key bends around the circumference. Every so often he would hold it up to the light, turning, adjusting, and bending again until he got it just right. Finally, at the base was the pull tab and he pinched it to display his creation to Bear: a star.

"For the tree," said Kris. "See? A North Star."

Kris got up and secured the makeshift tree topper to the sapling. It was crude and uneven, mottled at best. But it worked. The expiration date stared back at him. He returned to sit beside Bear and collected the small paper wrapper from the tin can. He began folding and creasing it in a series of practiced movements until the flat wrapper evolved into a paper crane. When finished, he set it on the sapling, balled his fists, stretched his fingers, and rubbed his joints.

The paka-paka erupted again in the east, but much closer this time. Bear looked to Kris, his ears pinned back, then looked toward the noise. The sound of a diesel truck fired up and droned in the distance. Kris began adding more wood to the fire, knowing his next meal was depending on it. A few of the branches weren't as dry as he'd thought, and they sent up a plume of gray smoke. He shuffled and looked upward as it crested beyond the treetops around him. He stirred the fire and added some tinder until the smoke dissipated, hoping his mistake didn't give away his position. A few more rocks. A few more sticks. Keep it hot.

Kris took a swig from his canteen and poured the rest into his container. Then, he added the pheasant feet to the container and started moving aside rocks to place it on the coals. As the water began to boil, he reached into his bag and pulled out another small tin.

Inside, a series of seasonings sat ready to contribute. A few peppercorns, a little salt, some dried spices he'd collected along the way. Stirring the feet and adding spice or snow as he went, Kris paused only to lift a makeshift serving spoon of the broth to his mouth, testing it from time to time. As it finished up, he pulled the container and set it in the snow to cool. He laid back, his eyes to the sun, feeling the faint heat on the back of his eyelids.

Kris awakened at the sound of a snap. A twig broke at the edge of the grove. Then again. Snap. Bear was already on it, ears perked and his nape on edge. Kris began snapping his fingers and gave a hand signal, calling the dog closer, into the tree shelter. Too late for the fire, quiet the dog. Bear withdrew, obedient, but confused. Kris drew him in closer and kneeled, his back to the entryway and Bear at his chest.

A single set of footsteps approached. The familiar crunch of snow beneath a heavy boot. Then again. Crunch. The steps got closer and closer. Bear began to growl.

"I see you in there!" the voice called out. "Get your hands up!"

Kris raised his hands and Bear poked his head around to see. His growl got louder and his hair stood on end, as he bared his teeth.

"I'm just an old man, I'm not worth the bullet, or the memory."

The soldier dropped his sight, lowering the barrel just slightly away from the old man to get a better look. Kris slowly moved one of his raised hands to point at the makeshift Christmas tree.

"What's this all about?" the soldier asked.

Kris looked back at the soldier. He was dressed head to toe in tactical gear. The hard lines at the edge of his eyes softened ever so slightly as he realized what the sapling was showing him.

"It's Christmas, boy." Kris said, confused that he had to explain. "At ease. I mean you no harm."

The soldier snapped his rifle back up. "You keep that dog under wraps, you hear?"

"Scouts honor," Kris said, raising three fingers.

The soldier began to ease. He approached the fire and lowered his rifle, kneeling down to warm his hands. Kris lowered his arms and turned toward the soldier at his fire. He shushed Bear's growl.

"You must have a death wish, out here in the cold on your own old man."

"Ain't got any place else to go," Kris said. "But I ain't alone, either."

Kris patted Bear on the back and Bear broke his gaze from the soldier.

"So, you're just out here having the time of your life, then, huh?"

"Not exactly," Kris said. "Just trying to have a moment of peace. I'm about to have me a fine dinner. You're welcome to join me if you can set that rifle aside for a beat."

"Sure," he said. "No problem. I'll just set aside my firearm for your imaginary meal. Where is it, now? In the oven there by your little Christmas tree? Give me a break."

"It's right in front of you," Kris said. "You've just got to know where to look."

"You're right, old man, it's not worth the bullet," said the soldier. "And from the sound of it you're a bit crazy in the head. But I wouldn't mind stealing a little warmth from your fire if you don't mind. Then I'll be on my way."

The soldier set his rifle aside, leaning it against a tree nearby, yet well within reach. He removed a small pouch from his thigh pocket and began to open it. Bear perked up at the sound of a foil package being opened. He began sniffing the air and taking little steps closer. The soldier offered up a small chunk and Bear stepped closer. He looked back at Kris for approval and with a nod, the dog carefully accepted the food.

"He seems to be eating all right," the soldier said. "So, where's this massive feast?"

Kris pointed at the fire. "It's right in front of your face."

The soldier shook his head and took a drink from a canteen at his side. Kris approached the fire and began moving the rocks aside. He jerked back from the heat and tried kicking the stones instead. The soldier watched in silence as he worked, offering no help.

"You got a decent shovel in that mess of yours?" Kris asked.

The soldier produced a small collapsible shovel and tossed it over the fire to Kris. "Don't get any ideas."

Kris unfolded the shovel and started again. One by one, he'd pull a rock and add it to a new ring next to the fire pit. Then he'd move the coals over to the bed of the new fire pit. After adding a few more logs, he got the fire going strong again.

Then he started to move the ash and coals aside. When he reached the layer of leaves, they began to steam, and the aroma of roasted pheasant started to break free. He moved aside a few leaves and looked up at the soldier. The soldier was looking back at him in amazement.

"You sure you don't want to join me?" Kris asked, smirking a bit.

The soldier smiled for the first time, and Kris pulled the rest of the bird out. He set it on a row of sticks on his pile of ash and dirt. The bird was crisp on the outside and dripped with grease from beneath, searing and hissing as it fell onto the ash.

Kris sliced off a section of leg and offered it up to the soldier. He accepted it and for just a moment, he closed his eyes to smell that foreign hint of a home cooked meal. He took a slow bite and began to nod. Kris sliced off another piece and offered it up to Bear. Then, he collected a small portion for himself and sat back near the new fire.

The soldier produced a small package of crackers and a cheese spread. Kris watched as the soldier worked and noticed how his hands moved with the ease of youth. The soldier offered up a few sections of the cracker and Kris accepted. He gave the package to Bear, who began licking it clean.

"It's not a pheasant, but it's all I have at the moment," the soldier offered.

They ate in silence, strangers in the snow. And they watched as the fire grew and faded, churning away at the fuel. Eventually, the bird was reduced to bones and Kris collected the carcass and separated the bones for later use.

"What did you do before the war?" the soldier asked as he watched Kris working.

"I was a mason," he replied. "Chimneys and

such."

"You ever serve?"

"I had my time. That was a long time ago."

"I'm sure you could still shoulder a rifle though," the soldier returned. "You could head back with me. We've got food. Shelter."

"I imagine I could if I wanted to. But then I wouldn't be here, now, would I?"

"I see. No more fight left in you, huh?"

"The fight is still in me," Kris said. "It's just a different kind."

"Do you think this will ever end?" the soldier asked, putting snow into his canteen.

"I guess that's up to you."

The soldier looked back at the fire.

Kris reached for a round of wood and added it to the coals.

"It's hard for me to look back and unsee what I've seen," Kris said. "I've been where you are. We're ages apart, but not that different if you think about it. You just haven't seen as much yet."

"Guess so."

Bear stood, stretched, circled, then laid back down again as both men watched in silence.

"It's a nice fire," Kris said without looking away from the flames.

The soldier nodded. He stood in silence for a moment and looked up at the small sapling, then stood and walked closer to it.

"I didn't notice your little bird on this tree until just now."

"It's a crane," Kris said.

"Huh. Why a crane?"

Kris broke his gaze from the fire to look at the soldier. "It's a symbol of peace."

"Just looks like a regular old bird to me," he replied.

"Peace means something different to everyone," Kris said. "Sometimes you need to appreciate it for what it is while you can."

The soldier nodded. Several silent minutes passed, with the exception of a crackle or pop from the flames and an ember dancing skyward. The violet hue of sunset beckoned on the horizon.

"I have to report back, or they'll send out a search party."

Kris nodded. "Going to tell them about me?"

"Maybe. Just an old man and his dog, waiting to die."

"Fair enough."

The soldier rummaged through his vest and pulled out a small shiny package and a bottle. He offered it up to Kris. Kris accepted it, opening his hand to see a small bar of chocolate and an airplane bottle of southern whiskey. Kris' eyes lit up and he looked back at the soldier.

"For your hospitality," the soldier said. "Merry Christmas."

Kris got up and collected the small origami crane from the tree, flattened it and handed it to the soldier.

"And to you."

The soldier stood and gathered his rifle from the tree where it waited, then shouldered it before turning to leave. He put the crane in a small pocket in his vest and looked back to give the old man a nod. Kris and

Bear watched him as he returned to the path he came in on, retracing his footsteps. Bear took a station next to Kris and sat down. Together, they watched as he marched away, crunching through the snow.

"I think he'll be all right," Kris said, looking down at Bear.

Bear wagged his tail slowly. A good sign.

About the Author — D. Ryan Buford

Ryan Buford is a native of the Pacific Northwest and currently resides somewhere on the Palouse – a region spreading between eastern Washington and the lower half of North Idaho.

Two years ago, he left the city/suburban life in search of greater purpose and meaningful lifestyle. From the outside he had it all – a reasonable house, a good job in the construction/demolition industry, happy kids and a solid path. But with the explosion of houses and population nearby, the encroachment of people was becoming more and more apparent. Houses clustered in serpentine streets were being built (and still are) directly above a shared water source that over time can only sustain so much. The land used for development was mostly farmland that in decades past helped to recharge the aquifer below. And feed families above.

Looming fears of water contamination, overpopulation, unsustainable growth, various natural disasters and a general lack of confidence in the human condition ignited the move to a simpler life with a little bit of elbow room.

But with that move came a distinct realization: every day skills once commonplace in his own family history not two generations removed have been all but lost. Even with a wealth of knowledge on the construction industry side, few skills transferred over to self-sustainability. Now, he's on a mission to restore these skills and infuse them in his own children, friends, and family. Maintaining a homestead has been a full-time job, but it is a wealth of knowledge and opportunity when it comes to harnessing the basic skills for survival – a wealth of knowledge that he hopes to inspire with every story.

CHAPTER 9 — BART

It was a dark and stormy day, with the wind howling ferociously, while the huge flakes of snow pelted the front window in the cabin. Bart stared out into the maelstrom and slowly shook his head. He admitted to himself that this wasn't an ordinary storm. He remembered that the weather forecaster on the radio had called it a 'snowcalypse,' which was a portmanteau of the words snow and apocalypse. Bart wondered, though, how a snowstorm, even an intense one such as was currently occurring, could be called an apocalypse.

The intensity of the storm was something he had never witnessed before, which was saying something, given his 60 years of age. Bart remembered the one winter when the temperature had fallen to minus 50 degrees Fahrenheit. The weather wasn't usually that extreme on his small ranch outside of Eureka, Montana. But he know that the extreme winter weather could come barreling down from Canada.

Still, usually when the weather was that cold, there wasn't enough moisture in the air to produce very much snow. But this storm was obviously an exception, with record low temperatures and an extreme amount of snow.

Bart grabbed another piece of firewood and tossed it into his black woodstove. The cabin was well insulated, but with the extreme amount of wind in the storm, the interior temperature was beginning to drop. Fortunately, Bart had known of the storm's approach and had brought several loads of firewood into the cabin. At least he could keep the stove fed a steady diet of seasoned and dried wood without having to go outside into the storm.

As the lights flickered twice and then went out, Bart sighed deeply. Power outages weren't uncommon in the northern reaches of Montana, especially in winter when the storms hit. Sometimes, they only lasted for a few hours until the linemen could get out and repair the damaged lines. However, Bart expected that this outage would take much longer to repair, given the way the snow was drifting. He guessed that it could be several weeks, or maybe even a month or two, before the road crews could get the roads plowed so that the electric company could get their trucks in to fix the damage. Still, Bart wasn't worried, given that he had supplied himself well with food, firewood, water, and all of the other necessities of life.

Bart eyed the woodstove, the cheery red glow from the fire shining through the Pyrex glass in the door. He knew that the stove would continue to produce heat, even with the electricity out, but he worried about how well that heat would be distributed around the small cabin. Fortunately, he had a small, heat-driven fan sitting on top of the stove. It converted heat from the stove into electricity, which was then used to turn a small fan. The small fan was still spinning rapidly, and he could feel the warm breeze coming from it.

Despite it being almost noon, the inside of the cabin was quite dark, which was a testament to the intensity of the storm. Bart had several kerosene lanterns spaced around the main room of the cabin, along with enough kerosene to last for many months of continuous use. Slowly, he rose from his seat and rubbed his arthritic hands before making his way into the kitchen portion of the cabin. Once in the kitchen, he obtained a box of kitchen matches, which he used to light several of the lamps.

"Uncle Bart, did you know the electricity is out?" asked Maria, as she stepped out of the bedroom and past the tiny Christmas tree, which Bart had erected. This was the first year he'd put up a Christmas tree in over 40 years, but this was also the first year that he wouldn't be spending Christmas by himself.

Bart nodded in response, "Yep, happens almost every time we have a winter storm."

"Ok." chuckled Maria, as she struggled to pull a pink snow suit onto the brown stuffed bear she was carrying. "We'll be out in a few minutes to fix some lunch."

"Take your time." smiled Bart.

Bart wasn't really used to having anyone else in the cabin with him. He supposed that he might be called a hermit by most people. But while he didn't necessarily hate other people, he just found life easier if he could do things on his own schedule and in his own way, with no one interfering, or interrupting him to tell him of a supposedly better way. He had been what he described as 'comfortable' while living by himself.

Of course, all good things come to an end, and that had been the case when his brother had died back in the summer. Bart's brother was considerably younger than he was, but heart attacks can happen at any age, or so his brother's doctor had told him. Sadly, the heart attack had happened at the worst possible moment, as his brother was driving on a narrow mountain road in northern Arizona. When the heart attack struck, his brother's car, along with his brother and his brother's wife, had shot through a guardrail and plummeted 800 feet into the canyon below... killing both occupants of the car. This was how Bart came to be appointed as Maria's guardian.

Maria wasn't a bad kid, well, at least for a 16-year-old young lady. But living with a 16-year-old young lady had taken a lot of getting used to, especially in a cabin designed for only one person. Obviously, she needed privacy, which was how Bart lost his bedroom and was forced to sleep on the sofa in the main room. Still, Bart didn't really mind since the sofa was quite comfortable and was closer to the woodstove.

What Bart wasn't so thrilled with is that Maria had invited her aunt, Bonnie, up for a visit. Bonnie was his brother's wife's younger sister. Bart had cautioned her that the weather could turn nasty, but Maria didn't have any concept of what nasty weather meant. After all, Maria had grown up in Arizona, where nasty weather meant a hot, dry wind. And, Maria's aunt had lived most of her life in Los Angeles, which was about as different from northern Montana as could be.

What was even worse is that Bart had a suspicion that Maria was trying to play matchmaker between himself and her aunt, despite her best efforts to keep that secret. After all, Maria's aunt was only 35 years of age and had been single for her entire life. He had even overheard some phone calls between Maria and Bonnie, where they had been discussing Bonnie's dating problems in Los Angeles.

Still, Bart knew that Maria needed to stay in contact with the few people left in her family, with those being only Bart and Bonnie. And, Bart was painfully aware of how little social interaction Maria had, given the remoteness of his cabin. Plus, he wanted to ensure that Maria had a woman's influence readily available. Still, Maria had settled in about as well as could have been expected and she was delighted to work with the animals on Bart's small ranch. She had readily made friends with his old horse, Joe, and regularly took him out riding in the valleys between the mountains. And, she had even calmed his small herd of goats. Her thrill at collecting a basket of eggs from his chickens was just pure joy.

In any case, Bonnie had arrived in Eureka several days earlier, where Bart had met her and led her back to his cabin. Bart had to suppress a strong urge to snort derisively when he noticed that she was driving a Smart car. Unable to resist, he initially indicated that it might be easier to just load her car up into the back of his pickup truck and haul it up to his ranch, but when Bonnie scowled, he backed off of the idea. Still, while he acknowledged that the tiny vehicle obtained some excellent fuel economy, he wondered how well suited it would be to driving in northern Montana, especially in the winter. He'd just added more gravel to his long driveway and had used his tractor to smooth it out, so he hoped that the small car wouldn't bottom out in any potholes.

Meanwhile, Maria bubbled rapidly about how great life on the ranch was and what a great opportunity it was for someone to connect with nature. Bart wasn't sure, but he thought he noticed Bonnie frowning a time or two as Maria went through the various rustic appliances and features of the cabin. Bart was, of course, completely happy with the way he had furnished his cabin and didn't mind the occasional visitor, but he had certainly convinced himself that he wasn't going to change his cabin for anyone. Still, he thought he noticed a note of conspiracy circulating between Maria and Bonnie.

Bart had consoled himself that Bonnie would only be visiting for a week. Her Christmas vacation was only two weeks long, and accounting for the drive up from Los Angeles and the drive back, he knew that she'd only have a week to spend at his cabin with Maria. However, as he glanced back out the window and noticed the snow drifting ever higher, he began to wonder how long Bonnie would be staying with them. After all, there was no way that her Smart car would make it through the drifts.

Bart sighed audibly. It wasn't that he didn't like Bonnie. She was certainly a very attractive lady. And, while the clothing she typically wore exposed a lot more skin than he was used to seeing, especially in northern Montana, and especially in winter, he had to admit that she was put together quite nicely. Still, he reminded himself that he was sixty years of age and there was no way that he should be romantically interested in a lady who was only 35 years of age. And, to think that a lady of 35 years of age, who was accustomed to the rapid-paced sights and sounds of Los Angeles, would be interested in a 60-year-old mountain man was simply ridiculous. But despite how many times he told himself these facts, Bonnie continued to flirt with him shamelessly.

It was just after Bart had regained his seat in the comfortable recliner, which was strategically positioned in front of the wood-stove and straightened the bib overalls he was wearing over a red and blue plaid flannel shirt, when Maria and Bonnie came out of the bedroom. They both giggled suspiciously, as Maria pointed towards the kitchen area. Bart inhaled sharply as he noticed that Bonnie was wearing a pair of tight, black shorts, which exposed her shapely legs, which were on top of a pair of red, high-heeled shoes. A white blouse, which was at least two sizes too small by Bart's estimation, completed her outfit.

"We're going to fix some lunch, Uncle Bart. Is there anything special that you'd like?" asked Maria.

Bart stuttered, "I... I... I.... No, not really. I'd be happy with a slice of cold Spam on some bread. There's no need to go to any trouble on my account."

"Oh, it's no trouble, Mr. Bart." replied Bonnie, as she winked at Bart.

"Bonnie is an excellent cook, Uncle Bart. She's promised to show me how to make all sorts of wonderful dishes." added Maria, as she pulled out a cast iron skillet from the cabinet beside the stove and placed it on top of the electric range.

"I'm afraid that's not going to work, with the electricity out." stated Bart. "You'll have to use the woodstove to cook on."

Bart was sure that he noticed Bonnie grimace before she turned away.

"That'll be fun." stated Maria, as she grabbed the skillet and carried it over to the woodstove.

Bonnie followed her, carrying a serving spoon and positioning herself between Bart and the stove. Bonnie subsequently dropped the serving spoon and bent over to pick it up, which caused Bart to quietly gulp before he forced himself to turn his head. Still, the image of Bonnie, in the tight, black shorts, bending over to retrieve the errant spoon was an image he was going to have trouble removing from his mind.

Bart clumsily stood up and reached for his scarf. "Maybe I should go out and water the firewood. Err, I mean, maybe I should give some firewood to the animals. No, I mean...."

Bonnie turned to Bart and winked again, as she stated. "Oh, Mr. Bart, please sit down. I'm sure those tasks can wait until we've eaten."

Maria interrupted, as she smiled, "I can do all of those tasks, after we've eaten. That'll give you two time to get to know each other."

Bonnie started instructing Maria on how to make grilled Spam sandwiches, using a touch of butter on the bread. Bart had regained his seat and almost dozed off, when he heard the two ladies discussing dessert. Bart wasn't too concerned, since he almost never had dessert, but the mention of Bananas Foster piqued his interest. It wasn't until Bonnie had the sauce almost done, when she mentioned the words "flambé" and "Everclear."" As those two words bounced around inside of Bart's sleepy brain, he suddenly shot awake, just as Bonnie dumped the Everclear into the skillet. The sudden burst of flame when the alcohol ignited knocked Bonnie backwards, where she stumbled into Bart's easy chair and ended up in his lap.

"Oh, my!" giggled Bonnie, as she squirmed as she tried to climb out of Bart's lap. "I wasn't expecting that. I normally use rum, but well, I didn't have anything other than Everclear."

"Don't worry about it. Are you hurt? Did you get burned?" asked Bart.

Bonnie looked at her arms and felt her face. "No, I don't think so, although I'm afraid I may have ruined my blouse."

"Don't worry." added Maria. "My Uncle Bart knows all about first aid. He prides himself on being a prepper and able to handle any situation which pops up."

Bonnie giggled again. "Perhaps I should go change. I'll be right back. Don't go anywhere."

Bart watched as she walked to the bedroom. It was only as an afterthought that he looked at Maria. "You're ok, aren't you?"

Maria smiled. "Of course. I know better than to get burned."

"Good." grunted Bart. "Does she need any help in there?"

Maria shook her head, as she finished the Bananas Foster. "I'm sure she doesn't. She seems to know where everything is."

Bart blushed slightly, as he stood up and made his way to the heavy oak table in the kitchen. He hesitated slightly as he considered whether he should take his normal place at the head of the table, or whether he should offer that place to his guest. Finally, he decided to sit at the side of the table, across from his niece, as she served him the fried Spam sandwich.

It was just as well that Bart was facing away from the door to the bedroom, when Bonnie came out, wearing nothing but a floral-patterned bed sheet. "I'm sorry, but all of my clothes are dirty. I suppose I need to do laundry." she stated nonchalantly.

Bart gasped as she sat at the head of the table and one side of the sheet slipped slightly.

"I'd let you borrow some of my clothes." stated Maria, before she started giggling, "except I'm pretty sure you wouldn't fit."

Bonnie just smiled. "That's ok. This sheet is working just fine. And, I can do laundry after we're finished with lunch. Mr. Bart, where is your washing machine and dryer."

Bart choked on his Spam sandwich. After he noisily cleared his throat and glared at Maria as she started laughing, he pointed toward the back of the cabin. "It's on the back porch, but there's no way that any laundry is getting done in this weather. The water would turn into a block of ice before you could even get the machine switched on, even if you could switch it on, which you can't, because the electricity is out. And, we don't use a dryer; We hang the clothes out on a clothesline, but they'd freeze solid before you could even get them hung, that is, even if you managed to get them washed."

Bonnie smiled mischievously. "Oh, you're so environmentally conscious. I just love people who are environmentally conscious. It's so much better to use a clothesline, than to use electricity to dry clothes. Why, I'd use a clothesline, too, except they'd end up dirtier than when they went in, what with the air in Los Angeles. You know, for that matter, have I told you how much I like the air up here? It has to be a lot healthier for you than the air in Los Angeles. I hate the smog. You don't have any of that smog up here. You know, I think I'd love living in a place like this for the rest of my life."

Bart choked on his Spam sandwich again. After he cleared his throat, he sputtered, "But you have a job back in Los Angeles, don't you?"

Bonnie smiled, "Why, yes, I do. I'm a teacher in an elementary school back there. I just adore children. But I have to be back on January the second, which is when my Christmas vacation is over."

Bart nodded.

"What happens if you don't make it back?" asked Maria, as she glanced at the window.

"They'll fire me, and I won't have a job." frowned Bonnie. "But well, teachers are in demand everywhere, aren't they? Do they need any teachers up here?"

Maria smiled. "Oh, that's a wonderful idea, Aunt Bonnie. You could stay up here and teach school."

Bart choked again, as he suddenly realized exactly how a snowstorm could become an apocalypse.

CHAPTER 10 — APOCALYPTIC CHRISTMAS

It had been six months since the world as we knew it was decimated. I stood outside wearing my worn but cozy sweatshirt and old jeans, just breathing in the cool air. I was still having hot flashes and didn't want to get everyone else upset by damping down the fire again. So, I came outside instead.

Winter is a beautiful time of year, but it could still be deadly and while we had a devastating summer and autumn, I'd hoped to find a bit of relief this winter. I knew we would be working as hard, or if I was honest with myself even harder than before, but I felt like there was a slight easing of desperation in how we were all feeling.

It's done now, we may not like it, but this was how the world would be from now on, since the EMP or CME hit, and our country lost electricity, there had been terrible turmoil. So very many lives lost.

In the cities the devastation was unbelievable; planes falling from the sky, power plants blowing up, hospitals overrun... unable to keep the backup generators going, not enough trained people to help. Total chaos everywhere. Then you had to deal with the criminal elements when they came into play, preying on the weak and defenseless. Suicides were happening multiple times a day; people not willing to go on in the face of such tragedy, mothers and fathers losing their children. Families were torn apart when family members were out of the country or in a different province or state and had no way to get back to their homes. The elderly and disabled were not able to get out and scavenge for food. People that required medication. Most of the deaths happened in the first few months, then the ones who could get out of the cities with their families started managing better. Some found their way to small towns which weren't as crippled as the big city's had been. Some made their own communities with family and friends. Some stayed on their own and wandered from place to place.

For us, we had lived in a small town ever since my husband had died, the kids were just eight and nine years old then, and as I had never cared for the more stressful life of living and working in the city, I moved us, opting for small town life. I wanted to raise my kids in the country where they could appreciate nature more fully and enjoy the beauty around them. We spent every spare moment we had wandering around the small mountain area where we lived, enjoying the natural beauty of the forest.

"Mom."

I turned towards the door where my son stood calling to me. My heart swelled with love. He was only an inch or two taller than my 5-foot-6-inch height. Still slender, unlike his mom at all in that respect. His hair was getting long again... it's not as though any of us has had time to go looking for someone to cut all our hair, I have a habit. When my bangs start going into my eyes, I just hack some off with scissors and carry on with my day. Jacob just sweeps his up and sticks a hair thingy around it. Now, my daughter, CJ, would never be so crass. She still looks as good as she did before our world went to hell.

"Mom," Jacob called again.

I shook my head and headed towards the door he was still holding open. "You're going to let all the heat out, Jacob" I said cheekily, as he is the one who complains the most about the cold.

"I can't find the extra canning lids." he said as we shut the cold out.

"Dee thought they were in the space under the table, but I looked, and they aren't there."

"I don't think we brought them in yet, so they should still be out in the shed." I replied. I glanced over the table that was laden with canning jars that we had dug out of the shed earlier in the morning. The jars were piling up, on and around the table, as we had loads of vegetables to can. Thank God that we did. We should have enough between us to last the winter until we can begin harvesting the wild edibles that grow in abundance around this area. I thought again how well we did in choosing this place as our new home.

Dee, Jacob's wife, who had never wanted to join Jacob, CJ, or I on any of our camping trips with the little ones, had taken to the new world with determination. She was always there with a helping hand whatever it took. I watched her now as she gently took the dog bone out of little Mike's mouth and passed it back to

King without missing a beat. King ran to the door hoping for someone to open it so she could go out to hide her treasured bone before Mike took it again. Mike was CJ and Jerry's youngest, at two and a half years old. He will never remember what the world used to be like with electricity. Ken, Mike's older brother on the other hand, will probably never forget his beloved video games, as he is going on six. Carl, Dee and Jacobs youngest, at six going on seven, will probably remember a little more and his sisters. Jane and Lacey, being ten and fourteen, will never forget. I hope they will forget the aftermath though. My grandchildren will probably have nightmares for a very long time.

CJ came out with me and Jacob to gather the rest of the lids and anything else we think we could use while we finished up with the canning. Jerry was out hunting, trying to get a wild turkey for our Christmas dinner that was coming up faster than I would have liked. I still had to finish making gifts for the kids. Life without power still goes on, for the determined family. It took all day to cook, chop, and can the last of the vegetables. I sighed with relief as that was one less job to do amongst the never-ending work that it took to keep everyone fed and healthy.

Alan and Tommy came in from the cold with smiles a mile wide. Jerry came in behind them, and ran over to grab CJ in a big hug.

"You're not going to believe what we got" he said, grinning from ear to ear.

We were all gathered around them as they told us about the big moose that they were able to get. They had almost given up on getting any more than the one turkey that they had surprised, since most of the wildlife had been hunkered down with the storm that was coming in, when they came across tracks of the large moose. They followed the tracks for about 2 hours, but it had started to snow a lot heavier and the wind was picking up. They decided they'd better head back, as it was getting really bad out, when they heard a loud crack and they could see the snow starting to move down the mountain. The big bull had been trying to jump over a small ravine when the snow hit it, shoving it into some boulders that were near the bottom. Thank God, the men were off to the one side enough to avoid being buried alive. They quickly put it out of its misery and got it cut up enough to bring home.

We met Alan and Tommy at the beginning of the end.

*****

Six months ago ....

The noise was deafening, and we could barely see five feet in front of ourselves because of the smoke. The terrified wails of the little ones was heartbreaking as we struggled to find enough cover to hide behind. *How the hell did we get ourselves stuck in the middle of a gang war?* I thought to myself. I've never even seen a gun, never mind having a shooting war held in front of me.

"Jacob, we have to get out of here! Can you see any other way out?"

I could hear CJ sobbing in fright, as I cuddled Mike against the front of me so he wouldn't see the body laying out in the street. Ken had his face pressed against his mom while he shivered in shock. Jacob's face was pure white and his eyes as big as saucers as he told me that there was no way he could find. He kept looking at the kids and I could tell he was anguished at the thought that they could be seriously hurt or killed.

Jacob grabbed my arm, suddenly pulling me further behind the truck we were hiding behind. I, in turn, grabbed CJ. The terror I was feeling was building to a limit I knew would burst very soon. A large man suddenly ran towards us and ducked behind the truck where we were hiding. CJ screamed, and I would have joined her if I could have breathed in that moment of terror. He turned and looked at us while we huddled there frozen in position and swore violently.

"Get out of here now!" he screamed at us.

"We don't know where to go," I screamed back, startling myself by being vocal.

He yelled over his shoulder and another man, maybe a decade younger than he was, jumped in with us. "Tommy, get them the hell out of here." he yelled.

Tommy grabbed hold of Jacob and almost threw him behind him as he told us to follow him. He didn't look to see if we were, he just ducked down and started running to the left of where we were. We exchanged panicked looks and held on to the kids for dear life and ran.

*****

Present day....

When I turned, grinning from Jerry's news, and pleased with our good fortune, I glanced over at Alan and blushed as he gave me a quick wink. He did that occasionally; I think to just tease me or something. Tommy was telling Jacob how they almost got a bear, but it had taken off before they could get a shot at it. Oh...! That would have been awesome to have had. The skin alone would have made a couple of coats for the little ones. The fat we sure could have used too, but there's always another time. I was surprised it had been out in the snow and not hibernating.

We gathered around the tables to finally eat a hot meal of moose steaks, fresh from the grill. I took the serving spoon and loaded up the kids plates with veggies, rice and sizzling steak, as I told them to be careful. It was still hot.

I started to drag the big laundry tub out and told the kids it was time for a bath, needing to conserve water in the summer has made us conserve it in the winter as well, even though we have more with being able to melt snow. "Wouldn't hurt for the rest of us to grab a quick shower, while I looked pointedly at the men."

The guys had rigged up a shower that was attached to the cabin wall, so it shared some heat to keep the room warmer. They used an old metal container that had a pipe going into it from the stove to heat the water up. It usually ended up being lukewarm, as it was hard to keep it from being too hot for the kids. We had to add the cold water to it from inside the bathroom, but it worked, that's the main thing. Everyone that could, shared the shower. I think it was the guys idea with the wives in mind, to conserve as much as we could. The littlest ones used the tub, which we dragged out as needed.

Our daylight hours were pretty short being winter, so the kids usually went to bed easier than when they used to. Even without watching T.V. and playing video games, they were more tired since they all had to help out. Even Mike had chores to do. He was in charge of making sure his toys were put away. After the kids were tucked away in bed, the adults gathered around to discuss what the jobs were for the next day. The work never stops now, from dawn to dusk. We are probably luckier than a lot because we have some experienced people with us, but we are still kept busy just to make sure we can all survive. The amount of time it takes to make sure everyone is fed, with having enough nutrients to stay healthy is huge. We certainly didn't have this camaraderie or were this organized at the beginning....

*****

Five and a half months ago....

"URGH, do you want to be like Jerry? Running to the bushes every two minutes to lose everything in his stomach? Do you think that's a good idea Lacey?"

"I was only going to take enough to wet my mouth, Lacey answered, "I'm so thirsty," Lacey sounded so discouraged and aggravated when she answered back to Tommy.

We were all so thirsty and hungry. We had been only able to pick up bits and pieces of things to eat... and the bulk of that went to the kids, as they needed it more. But they were still hungry, thirsty, tired, and scared.

"Alan and I have told all of you, after Jerry got sick, you can't just drink the water you find. Doesn't matter that it's from a river that looks clean. You have to make sure it's clean."

We all knew Alan and Tommy were trying to help us. God knows they hadn't had to take us under their wings... and I am pretty sure they were regretting that they had. Most of us were clueless when it came to taking care of ourselves with no power. No more grocery stores. They were long emptied out, which meant no more packaged food and no bottled water. And also, with our family having been in the city, after school had ended... on a big, fun shopping trip... we had no home to conveniently return to.

When we planned the whole family going for a day shopping to the city, we had no idea what was in store for us. Never in our greatest imagination would we have thought that the world would end as we knew it.

*****

Six months ago....

Leaving the parking lot with the car and van stuffed full of groceries and bags of new clothes for the kids, we started for home. We had just pulled off the ramp that led to the highway to take us home when everything went dark and the vehicles stopped. Then the accidents started happening. We couldn't see anything, but we could hear it. Cars slamming into one another; suddenly the sky was lit up from a truck exploding when it hit the railing after trying to swerve around another stalled vehicle, which it wasn't able to avoid. Within a few minutes, as we were watching in horror, a plane fell right out of the sky — exploding on impact. Debris went everywhere, fire streaming along the length of the highway.

I blinked and things came back to me as if everything had been suspended in midair. I realized Jane was screaming in pure terror. The rest of the kids were all whimpering and crying not understanding what was transpiring all around them. Then I could hear the screams coming from every direction. I climbed out of the van and told CJ and Dee, to get hold of the kids. Jerry and Jacob climbed out also and Jerry picked up Mike as he hid his head against his dads neck. It was total devastation. I got everyone's attention, saying how we had to get the kids away from there. Everybody started talking at once, trying to understand what had happened.

"EMP," was what I yelled to get everyone's attention. "It's the only thing I can think of that would bring this much destruction all in one go, other than a bomb." I gave a big sigh as tears started down my face, "We are in big trouble," We have to head for home right now."

"What the hell mom, how are we supposed to get home? Walk ?"

"Unfortunately, yes, " I said to Jacob, "that's exactly what we have to do. There may be some cars that will still run... but look at this mess. No vehicle is going to be able to navigate this highway in a very long time and neither one of our cars will go. So, yes, that's the only way to get home."

Dee was crying silent tears as she asked, "How can we walk all that way with the kids Terry?"

"We have no choice, Dee." I said. "Let's pack up as much food that we can eat on the way, leave anything that we wouldn't be able to eat while we walk."

CJ spoke up with, "Mom, the kids cannot walk non-stop for hours at a time." She started crying heavier.

I closed my eyes for a second to get my head

back in the moment. "Ok I know that. I just wasn't thinking. If we go at a good pace, we can walk about three miles in an hour, so we could get around 24 miles in a day."

"With five kids walking among dead people and fires and screaming going on?" CJ sat on the ground sobbing her heart out.

Jerry went over to her and helped her back up, "What your mom isn't saying is that within the next couple of days, all hell will break loose when people learn what has happened. We've all heard your cousin talk about this stuff happening, well now it has. If we don't get on our way and get home soon, chances are we will never make it. It's at least fifty miles to get home. It's already going to take us a few days. We need to dig out as much food and any other supplies we will need. come and help me CJ."

Jerry led CJ to the car, and they started to unpack bags. Jacob and Dee started to do the same from the van. I gathered the kids up while their parents were busy and tried to calm them down while also giving them an idea of what was going on. Lacey and Jane were able to understand better than the boys. But the boys were ready to show us all how strong they were, and how much they were willing to help protect us and get us home. They all melt my heart.

Several days later, we were a bedraggled group as we reached a bigger town that was still miles from home. Everyone carried a pack on their backs made out of extra clothing that we stuffed with everything we thought we would need. We sure learned fast the difference between what we really needed, and what we thought we needed, from carrying the weight.

Jerry and Jacob carried the heaviest packs, namely filled with a couple of cases of water that Dee and Jacob always bought. I had always shaken my head, thinking why buy water when you already pay for what you get out of the tap? But I was thankful now that they did. Without water, I think we would have lost the battle.

We huddled together on the outskirts of the town. We weren't familiar with this town as it lay in a opposite way from the highway. As we were walking, we tried to go as the crow flies, straight along through fields and forests, instead of traveling along the highway. One, we thought it would be faster. Two, we wanted to keep the kids from seeing so much death and destruction. We found it was a lot slower, having to walk on uneven ground. There were also a lot more hills and obstacles, having to cross creeks and dodge a skunk at one point.

With several days already past us, we weren't sure if we should go into this town or not. Every one of the kids tearfully begged us to go in. Everyone was so very tired and sore. We finally decided on Jerry going to try and see if they could get a better look to see if there was anything going on. CJ was holding Mike as he slept, and she didn't want him waking unless it was really necessary. He had a bad cold and was feeling pretty miserable. We thought Jacob should stay also, to show anyone coming by unexpectedly that there was a man with us. One person should be able to be quieter also. Dee cuddled her kids around her, and they were all out like a light. It was a relief to unload our packs and sit on the ground while we waited for them to get back.

Mike woke and was feeling restless and uncomfortable, so CJ and I walked a little bit away so Mike and Ken wouldn't wake Dee and the kids. Jacob was pacing around, trying to keep himself from worrying about what Jerry would find. CJ and I were so busy talking about the kids, we didn't realize we had gotta further away from Dee than we had thought. A startling crack of a gunshot broke the silence. Ken jumped in fright and ran towards an old truck sitting at the side of the road across the way from us, just as Jacob ran into us from behind.

"Ken," Jacob called frantically, but Ken was so scared and disoriented that he didn't even turn towards us. We ran over to him, ducking as we did, because we didn't know who was shooting or where it was coming from. Shooting began in earnest as we cowered behind the truck. All of a sudden someone came tearing around the truck, stopping dead and swearing when he saw us.

*****

Present day....

"I guess tomorrow we will butcher the moose. Do you think we should can some of this one, or just freeze it?" I asked Alan.

"Wouldn't hurt to can some. Maybe about a third we could can, then I'll dress the rest out and pack it to freeze."

"Ok sounds good," I said.

CJ had gone out with the kids and fed Bessie and blossom, while the kids fed the rabbits and played with the babies. No matter how many times I've told them not to name the animals, they still do. I was pleased the chickens were still laying eggs in plentiful

146

quantities.

Dee had her list out and had checked off 'canning veggies.' I watched as she checked off 'Christmas dinner,' which made me chuckle to myself, until I remembered my own secret list of the gifts which I'd been trying to get finished for everyone. I had the scarf finished for CJ, but I was still working on the mitts for Dee. Socks were all done for the men, and the number of goodies I had been doing in the evenings when the kids were sleeping was growing nicely in the freezer out back. I had been so excited when Alan made up a freezer by digging a pit before the winter came. As soon as it had started to freeze, he would pour just the right amount of water into it until it froze. Then he would repeat it until a thick layer of ice had formed. With a few metal shelves conveniently placed along it, it gave smaller areas, so the meat froze quickly and evenly. To top off my excitement, I learned that Tommy was used to keeping bees. Having an abundance of honey was amazing, especially for secret baking.

I guess I was woolgathering. When I felt an arm around my shoulders I jumped about a mile, finding Alan laughing at me.

"I wanted to see if you would like to go for a bit of a walk" he asked.

I looked at him curiously but agreed.

We bundled up against the cold and walked along the path that led to the back pond. It was a beautiful night with the snow gently falling. "I've decided, I'm glad I didn't throw ya back when we found you and your family hiding from the gang that had taken over that town."

"You're just deciding that now, are you?" I smiled at him as we strolled along in the evening chill.

He laughed out loud as he grabbed me closer to him and gave me a big hug, "I think you're pretty feisty, Terry, and I would like to get to know you even better." he said, while wiggling his eyebrows at me.

I laughed, blushing again, and thought that was getting to be a habit when he reminded me about when we first met, and how they helped us get out from in the middle of a gang war. It took a lot of convincing to get them to assist us in getting all the way home since we unwittingly had gotten ourselves lost and we'd still had over forty miles to go.

*****

Five and a half months ago....

Tommy shook himself and stomped away before he said something he would regret. I looked at Alan and told him what I thought of the way his friend acted. He looked at me and shook his head before he too, walked away.

"Mom, don't antagonize them. I don't blame them for getting frustrated at us. Let's face it, the kids, hell.... We are all acting clueless because we have never been in a situation like this before. We're sick and tired of this whole 'end of the world' deal."

It took another two days before we came to areas that we started to recognize. When we came upon a barricade with a couple of guys we knew from town, we ran up to them, crying. They told us how the town had gotten away with not too much damage and no strangers coming through.

There had been a small plane come down, but the resulting fire had burned itself out within a day.

We didn't have a hospital in town, as we were too small to warrant it, but we had a great medical office with a couple of doctors that lived in town. We got Mike in to see one of the doctors and got some medicine to help make him well again. The mayor and doctors had a meeting with the townspeople, about how we would cope. They introduced an herbalist and said for everyone to start learning from our older generation to help make things easier. They were going to set up a community garden and with a few of the farms around, they had already started making both deals for food and helpers for the farms. They would need to grow, and raise a lot more, if the town was to survive together.

I was very thankful we lived in a small town that was set away from any of the big cities. Jacob and Dee lived in town, but Jerry, CJ, and I, lived two miles out. First off, we went to Jacob's. The smell when one of the kids opened the fridge sent us running right out again. Several days without power in the middle of June didn't smell very good. We wrapped wet towels around our faces, and Dee, CJ, and I got busy cleaning the fridge and freezer out. The guys took everything to where the town was holding and burning the garbage in a controlled manner. That way we wouldn't be overrun with animals that wanted the rotten food. By the time we had the place in order we decided one more day wouldn't make a difference. We all crashed there for the night, after running over to the neighbors to get King back home. We were going to have to do something to thank them for keeping the dog this long.

While we didn't want to get up and do another thing we had to get back to our place and check how everything was. After we went through the place and emptied out our fridge and freezer, we were able to sit and relax before tackling anything else. It helped having the windows open, but I thought the smell will linger for a while. Though it didn't seem to smell as bad as we all smelled.

Alan and Tommy stayed with us while they helped, once again. They figured out the shower, that one had to be the best. Jacob and Dee showed up bright and early the next day saying they wanted to move up here with us. After being through so much, they wanted to stay and work together. We had a very large garage, as Jerry had been a mechanic, so we divided it out and made a couple of apartments.

Over time we traded for a milk cow and a few goats so we could have our own milk and cheese. We plowed the field across the way with a trade made with the farmer next to us, using his work horses… and in the spring we will plant more, maybe oats or wheat.

*****

Present day…

Alan took my hand in his and I finally felt like we were all home. Tomorrow we will go out and cut down the perfect Christmas tree. It may be thought of as the end of the world, but to me it felt like a new beginning….

About the Author — Tammy Fahey

Tammy lives in a small town, helping to take care of her grandsons. She also lives with two pugs who really run the household. Tammy has always been a voracious reader and finally let her sister Franny talk her into joining her as an author. This is her second story for an Angry Eagle Anthology and now she has a book available for your enjoyment on Amazon. Check it out.

Https://www.amazon.com/This-Apocalypse-Cozy-Apocalyptic-Novel-ebook/dp/B08HG2K8QD

CHAPTER 11 — THE TURNING

Days ago, when it happened, we had just sat down for a family meal. I looked up from the dinner blessing to find myself alone at the table. "Mom, Dad?" I called. No answer. Louder I called "MOM, DAD!" Shaking and screaming, "Where are you?" I ran outside. The entire street was in chaos.

That was the disappearing act. It was as though millions had been vaporized. Whoosh, just gone. Where did they go? Mom, Dad, my boyfriend. They were just gone. Where was the warning of this evil that had stolen my family and the people I loved? I turned my head, in the air came the mournful cry of a Whippoorwill. Had its mate gone too? Had the whole world gone wrong; or just my world? Had I gone mad?

Cars crashed without drivers; planes crashed without pilots. In the distance, the frightened howl of a lone wolf could be heard. A woman ran down the street calling for her children. A man sat on a curb, crying. The children were missing. Myra, 8 months pregnant, ran down the street. Her belly was flat. Had even the unborn been taken?

*****

Obviously, I did not go on the disappearing trip, even though, I was raised in a Christian home. I attended church with my parents, even became engaged to the preacher's son. However, I held a secret; I did not fully embrace the Jesus thing. I sang the songs, bowed my head, and talked the Jesus talk. But it was only a cover up. I did not think I was deceiving anyone. My only intent was to not disappoint my parents. Then came the world's great disappearing act.

I wandered aimlessly for a few hours before finding Delta, Wesley, and Shannon, my classmates, and friends. For the lack of knowing what to do we teamed up together. We decided to just live as we always had, at least until we could figure out what to do. At first the schools tried replacing missing teachers, but even that ended quick enough. We stayed in our houses until the water and lights were cut off. We had no place to go.

We became as nomads, just roaming, walking from town to town, always just on the move. It didn't matter where we went. We didn't know what else to do. Something about this time period just didn't sit right in my gut. We had offers to be taken in by government agencies, but oh... I don't know, it just didn't sit well with me. A little nagging voice warned me against going into the government shelters.

The first couple of years were not that different. Other than missing my parents and my boyfriend, life was ok. A new world leader surfaced, promising peace and a new life for everyone. He announced the mystery of the great disappearance had been solved. It was simply those people who held secret meetings against the emerging new world order had been eliminated, peace could now reign.

******

On this winter's eve, the gloom was so thick a pitchfork couldn't penetrate. This little group of misfits I teamed up with, stood outside the *Serving Spoon*. This was a rundown diner that had been letting us have leftovers their customers had walked away from. I was never into eating other people's food, but I was hungry. The world seemed crazier every day. It had grown toxic. I always thought Delta was a believer. She confessed she was just like me. She just wanted to fit in.

The evening was bone chilling and we were hungry and without food. The new world government had stopped giving handouts. We were all skinny as beanpoles. Wesley had always been tall and lanky, but he had turned into a freakin' skeleton. As for me, I felt and looked like a mangy dog. I had sunk to the bottom of the food chain. My entire world had turned upside down. We had to be on the move. Always on the move. It reminded me of the nomads of old. We were kind of like gypsies; except we didn't have a wagon to live in. That would have been nice. The world had always had homeless people, I used to just stare at them. Others were simply ignored; if one didn't see them, they didn't exist. The new world leader had declared that a little chip would solve the situations of the hungry and homeless. There were plenty of empty homes. Just fill out a paper, have the chip inserted, and a home would be given. Sounds simple, right? Something just didn't sit right with me.

We used an old barrel to keep a fire in. We had set up a makeshift home in a back alley. The rags we wrapped around us did little to ward off the frost. The cold penetrated to the bone. Worse yet, the wet climate made it seem colder. My fingers were so cold they burned. I had found rags to wrap around them, but they did little to ward off the frigid death. I stood at the burning barrel and sipped a cup of hot water. It helped; too bad I couldn't find a teabag. Why, oh why couldn't Mom and Dad had lived in Miami? I had to keep my humor, no matter how bad is was. At least fleas don't like cold either. I knew, without humor I would go mad.

In the city square the annual Christmas Tree sparkled holiday greetings. But it had become a Winterfest Tree. The new world government saw to that. They now celebrated Winterfest. The parades and parties, went on, just like old times. But was not the same. In place of Santa and his sleigh, we how had a statue of Nikos, the hero. Nikos, the one who saved mankind. He had put all the wars to bed; the world, for the first time, thrived at peace. Winterfest, the celebration to honor Nikos.

Adults ice-skated in the rink beside the tree. The laughter seemed foreign to my ears. The music kept time to the dance of the skaters. The façade of normalcy. Adults seem to have forgotten what it felt like to hold a child's hand and skate, or to read a bedtime story. The world was a lonely place without children. It seemed adults only cared about their own wants and needs. There was no laughter, no happiness in my world. There were no more children. The ones who had the chip lived a good life. This came with the new world money system. No one could steal your funds anymore. No more thieves. All of your information was stored in your hand. When shopping, one just swiped a hand over the light bar, then the transaction was completed. Winter lasted longer this time. My toes were turning blue. The rags didn't help.

This all didn't happen overnight. It was like the frog in a cold pan of water, set on a burner and gradually accepting his fate — without knowing he was being cooked alive. The river of change came in the spring of the new. This was an exciting time, yet a fearful time. Emotions ran rampant. This was a strange new world. Somehow, I felt the rapids downriver. Something didn't sit well in my gut.

We stay in town, at least we could raid the dumpsters. The Eagle had been replaced with a Bear. The symbol of the new world government. In my humble opinion it should have been a vulture. Everywhere was a picture of a bear, it sure wasn't Smoky the Bear. Even dumpsters carried a picture of the bear.

When the earthquakes finally came, devastation abounded. For once, I was glad to have been raised in a small town. No tall buildings. We moved around, yes but stayed away from large cities. When we were lucky, we found a barn we could sleep in. Some were working farms and still had animals. The smell of fresh hay and the warmth of the cows felt like a palace to us. I remembered Pastor John preaching on this time. He called it the end times. Maybe he was right after all.

Something or someone had to be behind this nightmare. I had always loved thunderstorms, but now I took shelter, when I could find it, from the storms. They were like no other storms we have ever had; deadly, with the white-hot hail stones raining down. The deep doorways were crowded with frantic homeless. I stood and watched an old man hobble to the doorway when a giant flying insect dive-bombed and stung him. It plunged into his shoulder. He screamed, and when he smashed his head into the brick wall he was only wounded. People didn't die. Some would try, but the pitfall was that death couldn't, or wouldn't, release us from the terror. It was nothing short of a bloodbath. The insects grew in number, the hail stopped, and the insects sought us out like piranhas. People rolled up like balls to avoid the peril, but all they did was target the back, the screaming was intense. The dive bombers looked like some monstrous genetically altered bug. They seemed to lurk and hunt. With each sting the pain, so intense the people would claw at the bite, but there would be no relief. Not only the sting, but the noise. Not really a buzzing… it was more like mini helicopters. The choppers grew in number. The whirling became louder and louder. People scratched and tried to cover their ears too. The noise was maddening. They were insidious and would not be smashed — believe me I tried. I ran like the others, another bumbling buffoon trying to hide.

Finally, they left as quickly as they came. Silence pervaded the air. Not a noise anywhere. No birds, not even a cricket. The silence was almost as insane as the whirling. Then came the aftermath of the attack. Within hours, pus oozed from the wounds, and the stench was gut rolling.

There was a tiny voice somewhere deep in my soul that pulled me into the past with my parents. It seemed a lifetime ago... but it was there, somewhere... things just didn't sit well. What was this tiny voice trying to tell me? It was hidden, but I felt it would surface. Something Mom had told me in one of our girly talks.

The world was being wooed by this Bear government, this One World social connection. The offers they made, like free food and housing, were jaw-dropping and mind-blowing. *One world government, one world money system, and one world religion. All one big happy family. MY FOOT!!* Something just didn't sit right. I was not buying this. I was beat down but for some reason I would not relent. I was not a gullible person and this insidious life had me in a tailspin I may never recover from.

Nikos was a breathtakingly handsome man. I watched one of his speeches on a department store television. His speech was nothing short of sensational. He promised the most inviting emotion. HOPE. The very air seemed to be hypnotic. Uplifting and amazing, the speech had many people falling on their knees in worship, right there in front of the screen. The nagging little voice kept me on my feet. The B-force came with chip guns and the promise: Once a chip is inserted, a home, and sizeable bank account would be given to start people on a new life. Many held out their hands and cried tears of joy when injected. I watched, my body shaking like a chihuahua. I ran away in terror. It felt like a trap. That nagging voice! I may go mad if it doesn't surface and talk to me. What was it?

Time moved on, sometimes so fast my head

swam and other times it crawled. One day the chip became mandatory. Where could I hide? Something was wrong. What was it? I was the only one left from my little group. There was no more group. One by one, the others had been blinded by the desire of food and warmth. They had succumbed to the forbidden fruit of Adam and Eve. Now where had that thought come from? Is this tiny voice finally going to surface? I remembered Pastor John talking about a Holy Spirit. *Remember, Ayla, remember.* Somewhere deep inside I know there would come a day of reckoning. If only I would have listened. Well, no sense crying over spilled milk. *Get it together, Ayla.*

I had been trapped in this holocaust. The tempting, stunning Nikos, held a strange attraction I could not deny; but I must refuse to obey. I had never been rebellious, but I was not willing to ignore a voice I could not call to the surface. I knew, without doubt, it meant my future. I, among, others in this unmerciful world were now being hunted by the B-force police. Anyone without a number on the hand or forehead were to be arrested and jailed. I felt a kind of deadly fear overtake me. The nightmares, when I did sleep, were steeped in terror. For some reason I could not fathom, I held on to the hope of the inner voice surfacing.

One day while digging in the dumpster, I was approached by two women, they told me they had been watching me for a couple weeks. They wanted to help me. I was scared, but I needed someone. I felt so alone and scared. My confidence in myself had been shattered. I trusted no one and it seemed they did not trust me either or were just overcautious. They blindfolded and led me away. When the blindfold was removed, I found myself in a large house. All the windows had been painted black. I learned they were covered in that way so they would not be detected as living here. This little group was part of the Resistance Network. I had never heard of the group before now. Each of us had a job to do. I was given the task of working in the garden. It was planted in the attic. It seemed a strange place to plant a garden, but it was a strange garden anyhow. Row upon row of plastic piping had been set up and the plants grew in water. Tomatoes, squash, green beans, potatoes, even cucumbers. My mouth watered just looking at it. I wanted to go into a feeding frenzy like a shark. My new-found friend wouldn't let me. She told me I would only make myself sick after so long of almost nothing. I needed to start slow, I would not go hungry again. After a vegan meal and a glass of water my 'new family' updated me on the world news. I had been so isolated I knew nothing, except to stay alive without a chip.

That night I was formally introduced to the group of resisters and accepted into their ranks. Then the Bible study began. Was I to lead a double life again? The meal seemed to have come with a price. Nothing in life is free, that has not changed. I decided to listen and wait for the bombshell.

"You do not believe?" Maria asked.

There it was… the secret had split wide open.

I looked at her, my insides curdled, with downcast eyes, the answer was forced from deep within my soul, "No."

Maria only smiled, "You will."

Maria become my best friend and my mentor. We worked together, slept side by side, she led me into Bible depths I never knew existed. The old saints became as friends. I felt their agony, defending and preaching the goodness of the one true God. The kings, queens, and slaves of the Old Testament became my friends. I felt as if I knew them. This new world Maria had drawn me into was beyond my every desire. Maybe if I would have listened to Mom and Dad I would not be in this mess, but with them. In my mind I laughed, better late than never. I felt like Alice in the rabbit hole.

I worked so hard in the garden; it had become my haven. My hope. Time had no meaning anymore. I was happy and content. What a wonderful illusion I allowed myself, but always on the lookout for threats. It was very real. We knew the government had drones looking for resisters. They emitted a small whirling sound, other than that, we never knew they were around. Often the whirling became so commonplace we neglected to notice them. We used candle power to bring light to the plants. I did not know candles could illuminate such growing power.

We were not so secure as not to be careful. We could still be discovered. One day a new man was brought into the house. He had been found lying in a back alley. Maria and Susan had found him. He had proven to be a good hunter and without detection had brought in meat he had trapped in the mountains. We had a firepit in the cellar of this old house. The floor was dirt and therefore not a fire threat. Smoke was trapped inside, but little by little it escaped into the outside in such small quantities it was not detected. However, once again, something in my gut didn't sit right. Who was this man? Where did he come from? Could he be a plant? He was a smooth talker, that's for sure. He talked of the resistance as if it was his own baby. He asked too many questions. He wanted to know if there was a way to merge with other houses. My gut was belly-flopping.

One day I talked to Maria. "I don't trust this new man. He is too smooth."

"Oh, Ayla, he's ok. I'll tell you a little secret. I'm in love with him."

"No! Maria, it is dangerous, I don't trust him. I'm afraid he might give us up."

"Ayla, don't be such a baby. He says he loves me. He told me I can trust him with my life. Look. He gave me this beautiful silk scarf."

It felt like a rock had hit bottom in my gut. Butterflies nothing, it was like those nasty insects were flying around in my gut. Strange the man had never been stung.

That night I left the house. No word, no note, nothing. I left as I came, with nothing, well, except a full belly.

I left the city; my inner self told me it was too dangerous to stay. I headed for the hills. I knew the mountains contained shelter. I would become a cave dweller. Talk about history repeating itself. Being raised in a small town, I knew something about country life. No, it was not easy, but I felt a little safe. I had learned something of botany in school and I knew some plants were used for medicine and food. Now, to remember which ones. It was spring and berries were abundant, but then, again I knew the bears would wake up too. I didn't know which was more dangerous: The city with the B-force, or the mountains with wild critters.

I heard a noise and ducked under a tree, watching as a helicopter scouted the area. The B-force was here too. I had to find a cave or something to hide in. I came across other people with the same idea I'd had... to hide out in the hills. This was not good. The B-force would come here looking for people. They were EVERY WHERE! There was no place to hide. I did not want to get involved with another group. I felt I would do better on my own.

Laying in a hidden thicket, I prayed as hard as I knew how. No response. The God of my parents no longer dwelt with mankind. We were truly on our own. I had finally conquered my passive belief, now a full-fledged believer. Was it too late? *Remember, Ayla, remember the sermons you daydreamed through.* I was determined to triumph. By some miracle I will see my parents again. Hell is real, this was just the forefront.

I laid there crying, I guess I cried myself to sleep. I felt a jab in my side. I sat up. The B-force had found me. Like a calf led to slaughter, I was taken into custody and placed into a church. Of all places I never thought I would be taken to a church. My fate has been sealed.

*****

So, here I sit in an old abandoned church. I am not alone. I look around at the half dozen people crying and of all people I spot Maria. She is heavy with a baby. The man from the resistance house is one of the guards. I knew in my gut something was wrong back then.

I went to sit with Maria. They have given each of the women a silk scarf. In front, where the alters used to be, is a smorgasbord of tantalizing food. Fans have been placed behind the tables, wafting the mouth-waters flavors to us. I feel like Templeton at the county fair. This is forbidden fruit which I must not partake of. I will NOT indulge. I will resist. I try to encourage Maria to keep the faith. Her spirit is broken. I don't know if I can revive her. There came bloodcurdling screams from the courtyard. We do not know what the screams are form. Wait, there on the wall, a screen and movie are being presented. It is of an older couple being led outside of this very church. There in the background is, *NOOOO* a guillotine. Well, this puts a different page in the book of life. Always one to search the brighter side of things, I think, *Well this certainly gives a new meaning to the phrase AND HEADS WILL ROLL.* I laughed and laughed until I cried with fear. I was a firm believer now and I knew my fate waited in the courtyard. I must take Maria with me. I held Maria and looked at the scarf in my calloused hands and, without warning, Maria jumped up and ran up front. She gorged herself on the food at the table. The man smiled, then came forward with the chip gun. Maria fell to her knees and lifted her hand. The chip was inserted. She wrapped the scarf around her head. Walking back to me, I saw eyes that were pure evil.

She stood over me and spat out INFIDEL!

Then, she was gone.

They are coming for me. Even though fear rears its ugly head and my gut is flip-flopping, panic pulsates through my veins, in the mist of this terror the inner voice whispers, *"It is well."* I use the scarf to cover my eyes. My knees are weak. I cannot stand. I shake uncontrollably, I know where I am going. I laugh, wondering if I will flop around like a chicken when chopped. It will only take a minute, but they drag it out. It seems like an hour. I am not resisting; I simply cannot stand. My legs are jelly. In hysterics, I laugh my way out. I have lost my scarf, but not my soul. *I AM VICTOROUS!*

About the Author — Conny Fuller

Conny writes Christian Fiction and joins us after her first book "Green Eyes" was a huge success in Christian and uplifting stories genres.

Check it out on Amazon

https://www.amazon.com/Green-Eyes-Angel-Walk-Book-ebook/dp/B07G66MXM2

CHAPTER 12 — THROUGH THIS DAY

An infant's shriek roused Valerie from sleep. It was the dawn of a new winter's day. Her shrunken stomach grumbled. She sighed. Food was the measure of each day. Every waking thought was on food. Everyday life was a battle to survive.

Bree, the infant's young mother, got up from the sofa where she had been sleeping and tended to her child, Roscoe. She gathered her son from his bassinet placed next to the couch. Sitting down, she nursed her son. She had him dressed in a fuzzy bear onesie that had little ears on its hoodie. The outfit was not only cute, it kept the baby warm. Although the suckling noises he made sounded more like a famished pig than an adorable teddy bear.

Slinging the heavy quilt aside, Valerie used her heels to collapse the footrest of the recliner to the normal sitting position. Her knees popped as she stood. In the months since the catastrophe, she had aged. Her hair was as white as the snow that blanketed the ground outside. The cold crept into her bones

The room had chilled overnight. The fire had died. Moving to the fireplace, Valerie squatted and stirred the embers. Adding a piece of wood that had been a neighbor's dining room chair, she watched it catch fire. As the flame grew, she whispered a prayer, "Lord, please help me make it through this day."

Valerie dipped a pan in the large rubber tote used to store water and placed it on the hearth. While the water heated up, Valerie slipped behind the blanket hung up in the doorway to shunt the kitchen from the living room. She went to the pantry aware the shelves were empty save a few items. She took two cans of cat food, pilfered from an abandoned home, and a sleeve of stale crackers. Apocalyptic cuisine left a lot to be desired. Placing a jar of instant coffee under her arm, she grabbed two mugs and retreated back to the living room.

Valerie was pleased that the water had come to a boil. Sitting the mugs on the hearth, she dipped a spoonful of instant coffee into each mug then added hot water. She pulled the taps on each can of cat food, opening both.

With Roscoe fed and his diaper changed, Bree laid him back down in the bassinet where he fuzzed discontented. She took a can of cat food, several crackers, and a mug of coffee and sat back down on the sofa. Crinkling her nose at the odor of the cat food, she said, "Yummy."

"Beats nothing," replied Valerie, returning to the recliner.

"I suppose," Bree mumbled, dipping a cracker into the pet pâté. She bit into the cracker. Crumbs dribbled down her shirt. She licked her fingers. Then with great care she captured each fragment on her fingertips and shoved them into her mouth, licking them clean.

Valerie watched Bree wolf down the unappetizing meal. It was evident that the young mother wasn't getting enough food. Valerie feared that soon the young mother wouldn't be able to produce the milk her son needed. After eating just a couple of cat food covered crackers, she handed the remainder to Bree, saying, "Here."

"Are you sure?"

"Yeah, I don't care for the taste."

"Thanks," said Bree. She shoveled the remaining kitty chow covered crackers into her mouth, devouring every morsel in mere moments.

Valerie sipped her coffee. The bitterness overwhelmed her taste buds. She made a sour face. It tasted worse than the cat food. She missed brewed coffee. But, wrapping her hands around the warm mug did give her a measure of comfort.

Everything had gotten surreal since Valerie's son, who was in the Air Force stationed in South Korea, had sent her an email. In it, he had urged her to stock up on food and prepare for an Electromagnetic Pulse (EMP). She didn't know anything about an EMP, but her son warned her that it would kill 90% of the population by starvation, disease, and societal collapse. Heeding her son's warning, she had stocked up on supplies before the power went out. It just wasn't enough.

Valarie glanced at Bree, who was now sipping coffee lost in her own reverie. She remembered how she had found a very pregnant Bree the day of the EMP attack, sitting on the front steps next at the house door crying. Her grandfather, Walter, had died. With neither cellphone nor car functioning and with most people at work or in school, poor Bree could find no help. Valerie had taken Bree home that night and the pair had stayed together ever sense. Walter had been Valerie's next door neighbor for years, even before her divorce. In fact the old widower had been quite helpful during that time in her life, checking the air in her tires and giving her produce from his garden. Most of all he was around if she needed him. Valerie knew the old man had a pacemaker. It had malfunctioned during the EMP. He had been found dead, sitting in a chair, an opened outdoor magazine still in his lap. When it became clear there would be no help coming, Valerie dug a grave in Walter's backyard. They laid him to rest there.

Combining the foodstuffs from both homes the women were able to lay low as society crumbled. After just a few missed meals and with no hope of the resumption of the supply chain most people turned violent. Many died along the highways and byways fleeing the city. With Bree in no condition to travel, Valarie hadn't even contemplated leaving.

A month after the world ended, Roscoe was born. Valerie and Bree both thanked God that it had been an uncomplicated birth. Soon after the baby arrived, winter blasted the stricken city with a freezing retribution. To survive the cold the women had moved into the living room. They shuttered it from the rest of the house by hanging blankets and quilts at the doors and windows, trapping heat from the fireplace.

"What's on the day's agenda?" asked Bree, interrupting the silence.

Her mind refocused on the present, Valerie replied,

"Finding food."

"Okay, where?"

"I was thinking about going ice fishing."

"What?"

"The stores were looted long ago. Breaking into our neighbor's homes has been less than productive. My latest scrounging effort resulted in six cans of cat food that we've almost finished. It's too cold to hunt, all the squirrels and rabbits are hunkered down, dogs and cats too. So I'm going fishing."

"Have you ever been ice fishing?"

"No, but I read about it in your granddad's outdoor magazines."

"You read about it?"

"Yeah, I read about it."

"Where do you plan to go?"

"The City Reservoir," replied Valerie.

Bree's blue eyes burned with incredulity as she spoke, "You know you can die out there from hypothermia. You could fall through the ice and drown. You can be attacked on the way to or back from the lake. Please don't go."

"And, Roscoe will starve if I don't."

"What?"

"You're not getting enough calories. Your milk production is decreasing."

Bree was silent, chewing her lower lip and avoiding eye contact. Tears welled up in her eyes then streamed down her face.

"So it's settled. I'm going fishing."

"Grandpa used to take me fishing. I should go," said Bree, wiping the tears from her eyes.

"That's a nonstarter and you know it," snapped

Valerie. Then softer she said, "Your baby will die without you."

"He's dying with me," Bree replied, sobbing again.

"No he's not and he won't. We won't let it," Valerie said rising from the chair.

She dressed in layers. Valerie usually slept in an undershirt and leggings. Since the EMP she had lost weight and had no problem pulling her jeans up over the leggings. A flannel shirt followed. It hung off her frame. Last, over her not so white socks, she put on Chelsea style boots with a thick faux fur lining.

Valerie knew she was out of her element, but she was determined to do all she could to succeed and keep the three of them from starving. She had already gone through Walter's fishing tackle, garnering the gear or close facsimiles to the gear the article recommended for ice fishing. She had read and practiced how to change lures and what to do if the line was broken. Placing the lures in a plastic container, she shoved it along with a Ziploc bag of artificial bait and few other odds and ends into Walter's military surplus ALICE Pack. She also packed a change of clothes, just in case. Plus Walter's insulted coveralls, thinking that she would want them later. It would be bitter cold out on that frozen lake.

In the second outer pocket Valerie crammed another piece of military surplus gear Walter had acquired. It was a woodland camouflaged poncho liner made from polyester batting encased in two layers of quilted nylon.

"I'm glad you found that," said Bree. "I know from personal experience how warm that Woobie can be."

Valerie nodded and packed a Buddy Burner. This piece

of equipment was something she had learned about years ago while serving as a Den Mother for her son's Scouting Pack. Her homemade Buddy Burner was made from an empty tuna can stuffed with coiled corrugated cardboard cut as wide as the can was tall. Then melted paraffin wax was poured over the cardboard for fuel. The cardboard acted as a wick. Valerie showed Bree the jigging stick she had made from a broken shovel handle just like the fishing article had suggested. She tied the pole to top of the pack.

Although Valerie didn't feel completely prepared for what lay ahead, she also knew there was no other choice. It was time to get going. She put on another layer of clothing. Over her flannel shirt, she put on a red sweater that featured a green Christmas tree appliqué. She had worn it to an ugly Christmas sweater party a couple of years ago. It looked ridiculous, but it would keep her warm in the frigid cold. She put on a girly pink sock cap and wrapped a matching pink wool scarf around her neck. Both she had knitted herself. Last, she slipped on her ex-husband's sandstone colored Carhartt coat.

Squatting next to the recliner, Valerie pulled a small pistol out its side pocket. It was a Ruger LCR .38 revolver. She had gotten the firearm from Walter as a gift. With a grin she remembered how he insisted that it wasn't safe for a woman to live alone unarmed. She recalled how he had taken her to the gun range to teach her how to use it. Pushing the cylinder latch button, she checked to insure all five cylinders had rounds. The revolver was light, weighing about as much as a can of soda. Its compact size made it easy to conceal in her coat pocket. She had carried it back and forth from work, secreted in her purse.

While Valerie was dressing, Bree heated up a pan of water on the fireplace then disappeared into the kitchen. She came back into the living room and poured the hot water into a thermos. After screwing the lid back on, Bree shook the thermos then placed it in the third outer pocket of the pack.

Valerie asked, "What's that?"

"Ketchup soup."

"Ketchup soup?"

"Yeah, from all the fast food ketchup packs you found at the cat lady's house."

"Oh, yeah, I didn't know you could make soup from ketchup."

"It's more hot water than ketchup, but it will warm you up."

"Thanks," said Valerie as she slipped on the pack. She picked up Walter's ax and headed to the door. Before opening the door, she gave Bree a quick hug.

Bree said, "I'll saw up the rest of chairs while you're gone."

Valerie nodded and stepped onto the porch. As Bree closed and locked the door, a blast of frigid air slapped Valerie in the face, taking her breath away. She pulled her scarf up, covering her mouth and nose. She checked the area for danger. Satisfied, there was none. She headed east in the bright sunshine.

The next block had been a combat zone not long after the EMP. She and Bree had watched from her barricaded basement as once friendly neighbors engaged in armed conflict over dwindling resources. The battle resulted in six bodies lying in the yard and three houses burning to the ground. Valerie lived in fear that she would have to kill someone to protect their supplies. But, after the big battle most people abandoned the neighborhood and no one else had bothered to come searching for supplies.

Valerie arrived at Church Street and took cover behind a snow covered car. In front of her was the Methodist Church. Early in the disaster it had been the location of a riot. A mob had descended upon the church's charitable food bank demanding its supply. It devolved into a scene of unrestrained violence. The once beautiful stain glass windows had been shattered. Valerie was surprised the rioters hadn't burned down the church. She turned south, heading to City Park. Now the wind was at her back, she didn't feel as cold.

Two blocks later Valerie crossed the bridge over Sandy Creek, which cut across the entire city. She paused at the bridge and watched the water flow. It was cold enough to freeze along the edges of the creek, but the water was too swift to completely freeze over. Valerie knew that once the snow melted in the spring the creek would be their major source of water.

Smelling smoke, she studied the clear blue sky for a sign of it. She didn't see any. Still it meant that there were other survivors around. The question was would they be friendly or hostile? There was no way to know. It was best just to avoid human contact all together. Sighing, she moved on.

Church Street ended at Morton Avenue, the main thoroughfare of the city. Valerie stepped through the shattered windows into the lobby of the bank building that stood at the intersection of the streets. It had been her place of employment on the day the apocalypse began.

Valerie had been working as a teller in this bank when the EMP struck. Even now, just thinking about that moment gave her goosebumps. Everything just quit. The lights went off. The phones quit ringing. The computer screens went black. For the first few moments there was an eerie calm as people tried to assess what was happening. Then without warning the transformer in the alley behind the bank blew up. Fire shot through the electrical outlets sending flames up the wall. Everyone stampeded out the bank in terror, customers and staff alike.

Upon leaving the bank, she found that her car wouldn't start. Looking around the parking lot, she realized no one's car started. In fact there wasn't a single vehicle on the street that was working. Valerie's fear turned to panic. She bolted from the parking lot running for home.

She didn't get far before a crack in the sidewalk caught one of her high heels, sending her skidding down the pavement. Cursing and rubbing her skinned knee, she got back up. Kicking off her remaining shoe, she headed home barefooted at a reasonable jog. She wondered if her shoe was still stuck in the sidewalk under the snow

Across the street lay City Park. Valerie thought about just running straight across and climbing the fence. Feeling the weight of the pack on her back, she reconsidered. She noticed the archway entrance to the park a half a block north. Her route decided she stepped out of the bank through the busted windows careful to avoid cutting herself on broken glass. Glancing left and right, she hurried to an abandoned car in the middle of road and paused. Looking up and down the street again, she saw no danger and continued.

After entering the park, she stopped behind a tree and examined the way ahead. She looked behind her to make sure no one was following her. Satisfied, she headed into the park. She noticed a couple of recently cut down trees, probably for firewood. Other survivors were about, but she saw no human footprints in the snow, but there were animal tracks.

As she passed the gazebo, she heard a growl and stopped. The sad monster face of a shepherd mixed dog stuck out from the broken wood lattice screen beneath the gazebo. The dog bared its teeth. Valerie hurried on, hoping the dog would leave her alone. It didn't follow her, but she kept looking over shoulder every couple of minutes anyway.

She approached the eastern entrance of the park and halted next to the brick and cast iron fence to reconnoiter. She had to cross Elm Street then travel east down Lakeview for five blocks to get to the City Reservoir. Surveying the length of Lakeview, she could just make out the frozen lake. The way looked clear.

Valerie reached the lake and scrutinized the area from behind a tree. It seemed clear of danger. Satisfied, she made her way to the pavilion. A compact car was parked next to it. No doubt abandoned by picnickers on the day of the EMP. She sat at a picnic table and rested for moment, contemplating consuming the contents of her thermos. In the end, she decided that she would need it more later after she had been out on the exposed ice for a while.

Valerie studied the frozen lake. It resembled the lunar surface, covered with numerous irregular snowdrifts and crooked patches of bare ice. The sight filled her with dread. She had read that ice was rarely a uniform thickness over a lake. She would need to proceed with caution. Unsure of the ice, she decided not to lug her heavy pack out on the ice just in case it proved too thin. She hid it in the car, leaving it out in open just didn't feel prudent.

She noticed some gray colored ice near the edge of the lake. It looked thin to her. She chose to avoid that area. Seeing some whiter colored ice somewhat covered with drifting snow, looked more promising. She thought it would be easier to walk on the snow than the bare ice. Carrying the ax and holding her breath, she took a tentative step onto the snow covered ice. It held her weight. Sighing with relief, she headed to the middle of the lake.

The snow had insulated the ice, creating porous air pockets thus making the ice paper thin in places. Valerie hadn't gone many steps when she found such a place. The ice made a gunshot sound then gave way. She fell through the ice. The shock of the cold water took her breath away. She hyperventilated. The pain of a 1,000 jabbing needles shot through her body. The pain forced her to focus. She had read about the 1-10-1 principle, one minute to get control of your breathing, ten minutes of meaningful movement and one hour before you become unconscious then died.

It took Valerie every bit of the first minute to get her breathing under control. Agony racked her body. Thankfully she was just in waist deep water. She shrugged out of her heavy work coat, afraid it would act as an anchor. She tried pulling herself up. The ice splintered and gave way. With chattering teeth she prayed, "Lord, I'm in trouble. Please help me."

She turned around, facing the way she had come. The ice behind her was still intact. It looked as if it would hold. Putting her forearms on the ice, she flutter-kicked her legs until her body was horizontal with the ice. Pulling and kicking, she was able to wiggled herself out of the water. She rolled away from the hole, saying, "Thank you, Lord."

Fetching her coat and the ax, she crawled away from the hole until she felt it was safe to stand. Her jacket was damp, but not soaked. She slipped it on and retreated back to the car where she had left her gear. The water in her clothes had frozen by the time she reached shore. Standing next to the car, she stripped her freezing clothes off. Her teeth chattered so hard she feared they might chip. She pulled the Wobbie from the pack and dried herself with it as fast as she could.

To get out of the wind she jumped into the car. Shivering she dug out her spare clothes and wrestled them on. She unpacked her Buddy Burner and with trembling hands tried to light it. It took her two tries to get it lit. In no time it had the temperature inside the automobile at a comfortable enough level that Valerie's teeth quit chattering.

To help her warm her core, she drank the ketchup soup. Wrapping her hands around the warm thermos gave her much needed comfort. She was tempted to give up and go home, but Bree and Roscoe needed the nourishment the fish would supply. Giving up wasn't an option. It took a long while for her to get warm enough to once again brave the elements.

Valerie got out of the car, grabbed the ax and headed back onto the frozen lake. This time she should would approach over the bare blue ice, hoping it would be thick enough to hold her. Every few feet she tapped the ice with the ax and listened, praying it didn't crack beneath her feet. It took a while, but she finally reached the middle of the lake.

Thinking that it might give her better traction on the ice, Valerie had brought the floor mat from the car. She dropped it on the ice and stood on it. Holding her breath, she swung the ax.

The ice splinted and cracked, sending an echo beneath Valerie's feet that sounded like a muffled gunshot. The ice held. She exhaled with a grin and swung the ax again and then again. It took time and effort, but the ax finally broke through the ice with a splash.

Valerie hurried back to the car, slipping and falling twice. She retrieved the pack and returned to the hole. She wasn't surprised to find a veneer of ice already reforming. Taking a slotted tablespoon from the pack, she dipped out floating ice chucks from the hole. Once the hole was clear, she shimmied into Walter's coveralls, enjoying the added warmth.

She untied the jigging stick from the pack. It already had a green and yellow minnow lure attached to it. Next she pulled out a Ziploc bag filled with red artificial maggots. Their unpleasant mealworm odor assaulted her senses. She baited the lure's hooks and dropped the line into the frigid water with a prayer, "Please Lord, we need a fish."

Valerie let the lure hit bottom and then brought it up a couple of feet as the article had suggested. She jigged the line, sending the lure and bait combination darting upward, then fluttering and falling. Again and again she jigged, trying to entice the lethargic fish to bite.

Even standing on the floor mat in coveralls she felt the cold creeping into her bones.

After a while Valerie felt a tuck on the line. She finally had a bite. Carefully, she drew back on the stick setting the hook. Hand over hand she pulled up the line, hoisting a plump perch out of the hole. It would be fine eating. Smiling from ear-to-ear, Valerie set it aside in the snow and said, "Thank you, Lord."

She dropped the line again and immediately got another bite. She pulled the fish up. This time it was a disappointingly small bluegill. Hoping for something more substantial, she rebaited the hook and once again dropped the line into the hole.

Valerie was ready to give up after a long time of jigging with no action. Then she got another strike. She could tell this fish was large. It was full of fight. She pulled the line hand over hand. The line zipped back through her hands. She feared she would lose the fish and her jigging stick too. Dropping onto her butt, she pulled with all her weight and battled the fish out the hole. With a cry of jubilation, she pulled up a two-foot long bass from the water. She figured it weighed a hefty 10 pounds.

Valerie was cold and physically exhausted and she still had to walk home. She gathered her catch then ran a cord through the gill and out the mouth of each fish, stringing them. After shedding the coveralls, she packed them then tied the string of fish and her jig stick to her pack. She headed off the ice for home.

Valerie thought about taking a different route home to avoid the dog at the park, but she was too cold and tired. Cutting through the park was the shortest way home. She was wary as she approached the gazebo. It still startled her when she heard the sharp burst of barking. With bared teeth the emaciated tawny dog exploded from beneath the gazebo charging her. Backpedaling, Valerie shouted, "Whoa, whoa, whoa!" The dog was only a few feet away when it launched itself at Valerie. The airborne canine floated by Valerie as she sidestepped the attack. Dead branches broke with loud snaps as the dog hit a woody bush behind her with a yelp.

Valerie sprinted towards the park's exit with the snarling dog in close pursuit. Looking over her shoulder, she realized she wasn't going to outrun the dog. The string of fish flopping on her shoulder gave her an idea. Without slowing, she loosened the knot holding the little bluegill. It fell into the snow. The famished dog pounced on the fish, losing all interest in Valerie and giving up the chase.

Valerie didn't stop running until she had crossed the street from the park and had once again taken shelter in the destroyed bank. She felt a stich in her side. The transient pain was intense. Panting, her breath made visible clouds of steam. After calming down she moved on.

The sun was fading and the temperature was dropping as she crossed the Sandy Creek Bridge. Valerie was cold, tired, hungry, and suffering a variety of body aches. Her situational awareness was nonexistent. She heard the sound of a shotgun slide racking. She stopped.

A bearded man stood up from between a couple of dead cars just feet from Valerie, aiming a pump action shotgun at her. He demanded, "Drop the ax."

Shocked by the sudden appearance of the gunman,

Valerie's entire focus narrowed onto the shotgun pointing at her. She didn't move.

"Drop the ax or I'll drop you," he barked.

Snapped out of her trance, Valerie let the ax fall. She pled, "Please don't shoot."

"Just do what I say. Now drop the backpack."

"But, I need it."

"I can shoot you and just take it," growled the gunman.

"Please, can't I keep one fish?"

"No, I got other mouths to feed."

"Me too," Valerie said, reminded that Bree and Roscoe were depending on her. A wave of calmness flooded her, tamping down her fear. She knew that only ruthless violence could save them now. She shrugged the pack off and held it at arm's length.

"Now drop it," demanded the gunman. His eyes fixated on the fish tied to the pack.

With the gunman's attention diverted, Valerie slipped her hand into her coat pocket. She wrapped her fingers around the rubber grip of the Ruger. She let the pack fall. Without pulling the pistol from her pocket, she pointed it at the gunman and squeezed the trigger. The earsplitting bang of the discharge made her jump. The muzzle flash trapped in the coat pocket burned her hand. The pistol's recoil whacked her fingers like a hammer.

The higher pressure .38 +P round torn pass the gunman's head at 960 feet per second. Panicked the gunman jerked the shotgun's trigger, blowing buckshot into the backpack and shredding the fish.

As the gunman racked another shell into the chamber, Valerie pulled the pistol from her pocket. She took a shooter's stance, aiming at the gunman. Her hands

shook uncontrollably. She breathed, "Calm down, be brave,"
Composed, she fired twice.
Both rounds hit the gunman center mass, devastating his lungs. His knees buckled. He dropped the shotgun and collapsed into the street.
Keeping the pistol trained on her target, Valerie advanced on the gunman. Looking down at the dying man, she said, "Forgive me."
His last words were muffled in a gurgle of pink froth bubbling from his mouth. He gave Valerie a pitiful look, closed his eyes and died.
Valerie wailed, wondering how many others she had condemned to death by killing their provider. Sobbing, she surveyed the damage done to her pack and the catch. The big bass had taken most of the blast. Not much of it was salvageable. And they'd have to pick buckshot out of the perch. After wiping away her tears, she pocketed her pistol and tied the ax to the pack and slipped it on by its one undamaged shoulder strap. After retrieving the man's shotgun, she headed home.
Beneath the light of a full moon, Valerie contemplated this new Hobbesian world where everyone was the enemy of everyone else. Life had indeed become nasty, brutish, and all too often short. She didn't like it.
She made it home without further incident. While Bree picked pellets from the perch Valerie warmed up by the fire with Roscoe fidgeting on her lap. As the fish fried Valerie whispered another prayer, "Thank you Lord for getting me through this day."

About the Author — C.J. Roberts
C.J. Roberts is the pen name of a 13-year Marine Corps

combat veteran who grew up on a farm in the Midwest and has traveled extensively throughout the United States and around the world. He currently lives in a small town where he is a minister and volunteer firefighter.

CHAPTER 13 — HOLIDAY TO REMEMBER

I breathed in a sigh of relief as I settled into my favorite chair. I'd been working non-stop all day making sure that all the decorations were up. Glancing around the living room, I had to admit that all the work had been worth it. The room looked like something out of one of Hallmark's Christmas Specials. The Christmas tree was a work of art! It was tucked into the corner where people passing by could see it through the window. Not that anyone ever passed by, but it was what I had been raised to do. Back then we had lived in town and everyone made sure that the tree could be seen through a window.

I wasn't sure how many more years I would be able to do all this on my own. This year was special though, the children had promised that they would be here to celebrate the holiday with me. I didn't get to see them nearly as much as I would have liked to. They were all so busy with their own lives now, and really that was the way it should be. I didn't need them worrying about me out here, alone on the farm. *Enough with the sad thoughts!* I still had a lot of work to get done if we were going to have the big Christmas dinner like I had planned.

I glanced out the window on my way back to the kitchen. The snowstorm the weatherman had predicted was going full blast out there. I couldn't even see the barn! I hoped that the roads would be clear enough for the kids to get through tomorrow. Looked like it would be another long day tomorrow. I'd have to get up early to plow out the drive, or they would never get their city cars up to the house. That could wait until tomorrow though. There was no sense in trying to plow now, it would just get filled in again. I had enough to do tonight to get ready for the meal tomorrow.

I grabbed the potatoes and started peeling them. Keeping them in the water overnight wouldn't hurt them and it would make one less thing I had to get done tomorrow. As the potatoes dropped one by one into the water, I thought back on other years. Things were so much better before my Walter died. We would have been sitting here chatting while I worked! Having someone to talk to always seemed to make the work go faster. I had almost finished the potatoes when the lights flickered. They went out and stayed out.

After so many years of living here, I didn't even have to think. My hand automatically reached for the oil lamp on the shelf. Within minutes, I had the lighter out of the junk drawer and had the lamp lit. *Well! This was going to make things more interesting for sure! Looks*

*like we were going to have a real old-time holiday if they
don't get the lights on before tomorrow.* By the flickering
yellow light of the lamp I finished up the last few
potatoes and went to get my winter clothes on. I was
going to need to bring in wood for the wood stove just
in case the power didn't come back on.

While I bundled up in my insulated pants,
winter coat, gloves, hat, and scarf, I had to smile
remembering how Walter had wanted to haul out the
old wood burning stove when the power line reached
us. I finally won that argument because the old fool
couldn't move the thing by himself and he was too
stubborn to ask for help. Good thing I had too, the
power went out a lot out here at the end of the power
line. High winds, ice, snow, or crazy drivers, it didn't
take a lot to knock out the power. Opening the back
door proved that I would have to do some shoveling
just to reach the wood pile.

Even bundled up like I was, it was a bitter cold
night out. My arms were aching, and my back was
protesting, as I hauled the last load in for the night. I
was glad that we kept the wood pile by the house
covered over with a tarp. It would have taken forever
to get the snow off it and get it to light otherwise. I
stripped off my winter clothing and hung it carefully
by the back door so that it would be dry and ready to
use again tomorrow. The stove in the kitchen didn't
take long to light, and it would give off enough heat
overnight to make sure my outer wear was toasty and
dry for the next day. With that taken care of, I carried
more of the wood into the living room so I could get a

fire going in the fireplace as well. We'd upgraded the chimney in the fireplace the year before Walter died. Now it had those new vents in it, so it heated the house better, and we didn't lose all the heat up the chimney. As long as I could still carry in the firewood, it could keep the whole house nice and warm. That had been a big help because the bills were lower when I used the fireplace to help with heat in the winter. It was getting harder to make ends meet with just me out here now. The garden helped with most of my food though, so groceries didn't cost me much. I still had to buy meat and paper goods, but that was about all. That reminded me of the meat I had in the freezer. If the power wasn't back on by tomorrow or the next day, I would have to can the meat in the freezer so it wouldn't go bad. Hopefully, the kids would be here, and they could help with that job.

Roger had called me earlier in the day to let me know that he was leaving and should be here early tomorrow. I still hadn't heard from Susan though. I prayed that they were safe and not out on those roads tonight. Grabbing a blanket and pillow, I curled up on the couch in front of the fire instead of going upstairs to sleep in my lonely bed.

The fire had burnt down to a bed of coals, and the house felt cold when I woke up. I quickly built the fire up again and went to change into warmer clothing. A look out the window on my way upstairs showed that the storm seemed to have died down, but it looked like it had dumped about two feet of snow before it gave up. First step today would have to be plowing out the drive. I was glad that Walter had showed me how to run the plow truck when he got it years ago. If he hadn't, I would have been stuck here on the farm all winter with no way to get out. Living out here on the farm could be hard enough without being trapped here for seasons on end.

An hour later and I was back in the kitchen, working on the bread dough. *So much to get done yet before they all get here!* While I waited for the dough to rise, I made up trays of cookies and snacks to sit around the living room. At least those had been easy to do ahead of time. Nothing beat homemade cookies on a cold day. The turkey was in the oven now that the wood had burnt down to coals. It had been a while since I'd tried baking in the wood stove, so I was really hoping that everything turned out ok. I punched down the dough and shaped it for the loaves of bread and some dinner rolls. While that rose again, I started on the pie crusts. I had forgotten how much work making a big family meal could be!

Just as I sat down for a break and a cup of coffee, I heard the sound of an engine. I jumped up and ran to the door. An old SUV of some kind was pulling in the drive. I didn't recognize it, but the driver was waving as he pulled it to a stop by the porch. He rolled the window down and stuck his head out. "Hey Mrs. Madison. I've got some passengers for you."

Just then the passenger door opened, and Susan and her two girls piled out. The girls ran up on the porch as their mother and the driver went around to the back. "Gramma! Gramma! We broke down and Mr. Wagner came and helped us!"

"Oh my! I'm glad that he helped you! That must have been scary!" Susan and Mr. Wagner came around the SUV carrying backpacks and suitcases. "Bring them in, you can set them down anywhere. Would you like some coffee?"

"Appreciate the offer, Mam, but I have to be getting home. The wife will be wondering where I got off too. You folks have a good day now."

"Are you ok, Susan? I was so worried about you kids driving in the storm last night!"

"We're fine Mom. Not sure what happened to the car. It just died last night with no warning. I just had it in the shop the other day too, to make sure that it was safe to drive this far. I'll have to arrange for someone to tow it to a garage and see what happened. I'm just so glad that we are here!"

"So am I. Come in and have some coffee and relax! The power went off here last night too. That was such a bad storm! We'll worry about your car later. I hope Roger doesn't have problems getting here!" As I led her out to the kitchen, I noticed that the girls had dropped their coats on the floor. "Girls! Hang your coats and hats on the bottom rack by the door. You should know better than that!"

"Sorry Gramma!" came back as a chorus.

"Susan, help yourself to some coffee, you know where the cups are. I have to check on the bread. It's been a while since I tried to bake in this stove."

The bread and rolls were done so I pulled them out and tucked the pies in to cook. While I buttered the tops of the bread to keep it from getting hard, I called to the girls. "Sarah, Milly, you can each choose two cookies off the trays and bring them out here to the table to eat. When you're done, we will get your things up to your rooms."

"Yes Gramma." I smiled, thinking that it would be easy to get used to that chorus.

Susan looked up and caught me smiling. "Don't get too used to that, Mom. They are on their best behavior right now. Normally they are little devils." she laughed. "It's so good to be back home. I don't think I realized how much I missed you and this farm."

The girls finished their snacks and we headed for the stairs to get their things put away. On my way past, I added a couple more logs to the fireplace so that it wouldn't be cold upstairs. "We'll have to be sure and bring in some more firewood before it gets dark."

We had just gotten everyone upstairs and shown them the rooms they would be in when a truck pulled up outside. "Looks like Roger made it!" There was a mad dash by two little girls to get to the door first. Susan and I were laughing as we followed them down. Our laughter died at the grim look on Rogers face as he got out of the truck.

"Thank God you're here, Susan! I was so worried when I didn't see your car!" Roger still wasn't smiling though.

"Roger, what's going on! Why would you be so worried?" Susan sounded as confused as I was.

"Bring your things in first, then we can sit down and talk about it. No sense letting all the heat out of the house."

That got a smile from Roger at least. "Still my practical and loving mom!"

I watched as he grabbed a duffle bag and

suitcase out of the truck. Something was off about him. Usually he was calm and cheerful. I dreaded hearing what he had to say. We sent the girls upstairs to finish putting their stuff away while we headed for the kitchen. When we were all seated with our coffee, I jumped right in. "Spill it Roger. What has you so upset?'

"You haven't heard anything?"

"No, the power went out last night and I was busy all day yesterday getting ready. What was it that I missed?"

"Mom, the power isn't just out here. It's out everywhere. They weren't sure whether it was a solar flare or an EMP attack last I heard. Just that the power was out all over, and most newer cars were dead where they stopped. No one is really sure what is happening, but people are starting to panic." Roger sounded exhausted. "I knew Susan had a newer car and I worried all the way here that she would be stranded somewhere with the girls."

"Well, you're all here safe and sound. It doesn't sound like there is anything we can do about it right now. Let's enjoy this holiday and we will worry about making plans tomorrow. I know that sounds selfish, but I would like just one more holiday to remember if the world is about to change on us. Can we try and keep this a secret from the girls at least for today?"

"Yes Mom, we can do that. I would like to bring in my guns though if that is alright with you. I know you don't really like having them in the house." Roger looked at me, waiting to see how I reacted.

"It's not guns that I mind so much, Roger. Shotguns and hunting rifles are fine with me. I just never liked the pistols. They are only really useful for killing people. Your dad's rifle is still in his gun safe. You can move that into your room tonight."

While I finished up dinner, Susan went to get the girls to help her set the table. Roger brought in more wood and helped carry heavy platters and bowls out to the table. The girls made sure every dish had a serving spoon, and that all the settings had napkins. The meal was a success and there was a lot of laughter and reminiscing about past holidays. When the table was cleared, we let the girls open their presents. We laughed at the presents Roger had gotten the girls. Each opened a huge stuffed bear. One pink and one purple, just so they could tell them apart. After the girls were tucked into bed that night, we began our planning.

Tomorrow we would begin to prepare for a new 'old' way of life. We were in better shape than a lot of people would be. I had been growing and canning food for years, Susan would help me with that now. Roger would hunt and do his best to protect the farm. We would all work on firewood and other chores around the house. It wasn't much of a plan, but we had no idea what it was we were facing yet, so it was the best we could do for now.

About Christi Reed

Christi Reed grew up helping her mother and grandmother garden and can. She can still remember all the hours of prepping vegetables to be canned. When her grandmother died, they stopped doing as much gardening, but those early memories stayed with her.

She's always loved to read and tried a couple of times to write but never had the confidence to do anything with it. She's 62 years old now and retired and decided to give writing a try again. Maybe this time, she hopes, she will have better luck.

Christi's works can be seen in the first Apocalyptic Winter Anthology as well as the Anarchy Anthology also by Angry Eagle Publishing

CHAPTER 14 — GARAGE

Samantha huddled in the small, frigid attic of the garage. She could still hear the feral dogs sniffing around below her, but she knew that they couldn't climb into the attic since she'd kicked the ladder leading to it down. Of course, she wasn't sure how she would get down, but that was a problem for some point in the future. She was happy, at least for the moment, being safe from those dogs.

Samantha understood what the dogs were after. They were after food of any sort. And they had come to view humans as food. After all, there weren't very many humans left alive. Not after the virus had swept through the population and killed off over 98 percent of the population. A small portion of the population, such as Samantha, had been immune to the virus. But for the rest of the population, the virus was lethal. It had begun innocently enough, with some sinus congestion and a runny nose, followed by a sore throat. But it didn't stop. It was a slowly developing hemorrhagic virus, which progressed to breaking down the tissues of the arteries and veins, such that people began to bleed uncontrollably. Samantha had witnessed her two brothers succumb to the disease, as well as her parents. Even her boyfriend had developed the symptoms and slowly died, no matter what she did for him. She had fully expected to contract the disease too, but she never did, despite caring for her family and being in close contact with them.

However, while Samantha had been inside, taking care of her relatives as they slowly deteriorated... until they finally died... the rest of society was rapidly disintegrating. Police departments, fire departments, ambulance services, hospitals, tow trucks, and just about every other public serving agency, had ceased to effectively function. In her small town maybe one member of each of those agencies had the immunity and continued to serve, but it was impossible for one policeman or one fireman to effectively serve the community. Plus, retail establishments were similarly devastated and ceased to function.

Burglaries of the now-closed retail establishments were where the wave of crime started. The surviving people needed food and supplies. They would go to any lengths to obtain those... including breaking into the closed retail stores and simply taking what they needed. But once the crime started, the surviving criminals saw exactly how easy it was to get away with crime. With that, the thin veneer of civilization disappeared entirely, and roving gangs took over towns. They claimed the supplies for themselves and enslaved the weak and defenseless. They violated many of the survivors in any way they desired.

Samantha had witnessed this rapid decay of civilization as she hid from the gangs. But she quickly realized that the gangs would soon be breaking into all of the houses, in search of food, supplies, or slaves. With that knowledge, she knew that the only way to survive would be to flee the city and go into the countryside, where the distances were too great to interest the gang members. But she also knew that winter was fast approaching.

As she lay on the rough boards making up the floor of the attic of the garage, she thought back to her childhood. She remembered Skippy, the dog she had as a child. Skippy was a brown and white Beagle and was always friendly to Samantha and even Samantha's friends. Samantha allowed a single tear to run down the side of her face as she remembered when Skippy had dashed out into the road to meet her, as she was getting off of the school bus one afternoon. He had gotten too close to the front wheel, which had crushed him. Samantha had never quite gotten over Skippy's death and had never gotten another dog, since she knew that it would be impossible to replace Skippy. But she knew that the feral dogs sniffing around below her were nothing like Skippy had been. The dogs below her would quickly kill her if they could get to her.

Samantha dared to look over the unprotected edge of the attic and could make out three large dogs below her. She quietly pulled back and laid down again. Eventually, she knew that she would have to come down from the attic. Hunger would force her to make that decision. But she had dropped her only weapon on the ground outside of the garage as she had fled from the pack of dogs.

The weapon Samantha had been carrying had not been much of a weapon. Before she had fled her parent's house, she had searched the house for a weapon. Her dad had been a bit of a hunter, but he had given up hunting after he had broken his leg a few years ago and had sold off his hunting rifle. And, he had loaned his pistol to his brother last year, too. A quick search of the house had turned up a claw-hammer and the broken wooden handle to a shovel. Samantha had used a rasp to sharpen the broken end of the shovel handle into a point.

The escape from the house had gone well enough, at least initially. Samantha had collected two bags of canned goods and a couple of bottles of water to take with her. She wasn't really sure where she was going, but she knew that she had to get out of the town before one of the gangs raided the house. With that in mind, she waited until just before dawn, then slipped out the basement door in the back of the house. She moved cautiously through the neighborhood, working her way toward the south, which was the closest boundary of the town. Several times she had to seek cover as she spotted gang members raiding neighboring houses, sometimes spending several hours hunkered down in places such as under the tarpaulin covering a woodpile, or behind the bushes forming a hedgerow.

At some point during her journey she had lost the claw-hammer, which she had slipped under the belt holding her pants up. She guessed that it had slipped out while she was laying under some of the bushes. But she wasn't about to go back and look for it. So, she made her way on, with only the improvised pike.

She wasn't really sure if she could actually kill another human if one of the gang members had found her. She had snorted derisively as she had thought of this, after realizing that almost all of the gang members were armed with handguns and could easily kill her from a goodly distance, while she would have to be quite close to impale someone with her pike. Plus, she wasn't sure how easy it would be to actually stab someone with the pike. She'd never tried using a pike before and wasn't sure if the wooden point would actually penetrate clothing or not. Besides, she had reminded herself… she was only a teen-aged girl, and a relatively weak and uncoordinated one at that.

The question of the usefulness of the pike had been answered a few hours later as she had rounded the corner of an abandoned house. Perhaps she had been getting tired from her journey, or maybe she was just distracted by thinking ahead. But she hadn't scouted around the corner like she had been doing. She had simply walked around the corner, coming face to face with a large brown dog which acted quite aggressively as it bared its teeth and lunged for her leg. She consoled herself that it had been more of a reflex action than a planned strike, but she had lunged toward the dog with the pike raised and pointed towards the dog's chest. The two collided and the pike had slid effortlessly through the ribs of the dog, piercing several vital organs. The dog had yelped once before it turned, staggered three steps, and dropped dead.

Samantha had felt a flood of emotions wash over her. On the one hand, she was terrified with the knowledge that the dog could have killed her. On the other hand, she was elated that she had defeated the threat so effortlessly. On the third hand, she was sad that she had killed a dog, as images of Skippy had flashed through her mind. She felt a strong urge to collapse and cry but she knew that she had to keep moving. With that knowledge she cleaned the end of the improvised pike in the dry grass as best as she could and continued her trip towards the south.

She was nearing the edge of the town as darkness was beginning to fall. She paused briefly to consider her plans. She knew that she still needed to get outside of the town; as long as she was still in the town, she was at risk of being discovered by one of the gangs. However, she also knew that she would not be able to navigate safely at night. While there was less chance of being spotted at night, especially now that the electrical system had failed and the streetlights were dark, she also knew that she wouldn't be able to see hazards. She could trip over or run into something.

As she was contemplating what to do, a dog howled from behind her. She spun around and was startled to see three large dogs heading for her. While she knew that she could handle a single dog, she also knew that there was no way that she would be able to handle a pack of three dogs at once. Her only option was to drop the bags of canned goods and to run.

Samantha sprinted around the edge of the house and noticed a concrete block garage on the other side of the back yard. She risked a quick look over her shoulder as she ran across the slippery grass and realized that the pack of dogs were gaining on her rapidly. Out of options, she darted into the door on the side of the garage. She slammed the door just before the dogs reached it, but luck was not with her. Despite having closed the human-sized door in the side of the garage, she realized that the door for the car in the front of the garage was open and that the dogs were approaching it. Unsure of what else to do, she bolted up the rickety ladder into the attic of the garage and kicked the ladder away once she had reached the attic.

Now, Samantha found herself stuck in the attic of the garage, with no food, or water, and with three hungry dogs roaming the ground below her. What was worse was that a cold wind was blowing into the open garage door. She studied the garage door. With the way the building was constructed, the attic only covered the back half, with the garage door occupying the front portion of the garage. She wondered if she would be able to push the door down from her position on the attic floor. While that would still leave the dogs down below, at least closing the door would block some of the wind from blowing in.

Samantha reached out and gave the edge of the raised garage door a shove. She was thrilled when it rolled away from her and started going down. But the springs then took over and brought the door back up into the raised position. Samantha consoled herself with the knowledge that the noise had frightened the dogs, who had exited the garage.

With the knowledge that her legs were stronger than her arms, she turned around and suspended herself on the edge of the attic. With some difficulty, she positioned her feet on the top edge of the raised garage door. Once she was in position, she gave a mighty kick and was quite pleased as the garage door rolled along the track and came to rest in the downward position. She was not quite as pleased with the fact that the inertia of her legs pulled her off of the edge of the attic and left her suspended by her fingertips. While hoping that the floor was clear, she pushed off the edge of the attic with her hands and landed on the floor of the garage. Unfortunately, her legs collapsed when she hit the ground and she rolled backwards, ending up on her back.

The dogs outside, upon hearing the noise of Samantha landing on the floor, growled aggressively. Having heard this, Samantha jumped up and turned the handle on the garage door, locking it closed. With that, she stumbled around in the now darkened garage and found the ladder she had kicked down earlier. She re-positioned the ladder and climbed back into the attic before pulling the ladder up after her. Knowing that she was reasonably secure for the night, she wrapped herself in an abandoned painter's cloth, which was stained with various bright colors of paint and fell into an uneasy sleep.

Samantha woke shivering and hungry. She briefly wondered why her bed was so hard before she remembered that she was in the attic of a garage, instead of her comfortable bed. She cautiously felt around and made sure that she wasn't too close to the edge before peering down at the floor. She could see light leaking in around the garage door, so she knew it was daytime. But she wasn't sure if it was still morning, or if she had slept into the afternoon. More importantly, she wondered if the dogs were still near the garage.

As she lay on the floor of the garage attic, she heard voices outside of the garage. Samantha jerked slightly as someone pulled on the garage door, before finding it latched and abandoning their attempt.

"Hey, Leo, quit screwing around with that garage. Ain't going to be anything in there that we need." called a voice from outside the garage.

A second voice replied, "What're we lookin' for, Bobby?".

"You know, food, weapons and, most importantly, girls," laughed the first voice.

Samantha shivered as she heard the response. She wondered if they would try to search the garage or not. Then, she wondered if she'd locked the side door when she had entered the previous night. She couldn't remember. She'd been in such a hurry to flee the dogs that she didn't think she had locked the door. She wasn't sure if the door had locked when she had slammed it, or whether it had just latched. She knew she hadn't turned the deadbolt on it, since there hadn't been time. After a quick debate with herself, she decided against trying to climb down and turn the deadbolt, since she was afraid that would make enough noise to alert the gang members of her presence. Instead, she just stayed, laying quietly on the rough wooden floor of the attic, hoping the gang members wouldn't search the garage.

Samantha discovered that sound carried quite

well through the uninsulated roof of the garage, as she heard a voice from outside the garage cry out, "Lookie at this, Bobby. Someone done left two bags of groceries in this yard."

As she silently cursed her abysmal luck, a reply came through the roof of the garage, "Someone must have dropped them as they were being chased by those dogs we killed earlier today. Ain't no tellin' where they are now, though. I don't see no blood, so they must have gotten away."

The fact that the gang had killed the dogs allowed Samantha to breathe a sigh of relief. She no longer had to worry about those three dogs who had chased her. But she wondered, how many more feral dogs were still roaming the town? She also wondered how long the gang members were going to be in the neighborhood. The pangs of hunger were growing impossible to resist. Samantha knew that she would soon have to venture out of the garage, regardless of what dangers lurked outside. Still, she wrapped her arms around her empty belly, squeezing tightly, as she bided her time. Perhaps she could wait until the sun had set. She knew that the sun dropped below the horizon at quite an early hour, what with the season being late autumn.

Samantha tried to sleep, but sleep did not come easily. She was quite uncomfortable on the hard floor. She was also cold and hungry. All of these factors made it impossible for her to doze off. She tried counting sheep, but all that did was to make her think of lamb chops, served on a bed of Basmati Rice, with a honey mustard glaze and with side dishes of boiled potatoes and green beans, accompanied by a hot herbal tea, ideally orange spice, while being followed by a thick piece of fruit cake for desert....

As she pressed her hands hard into her head in a futile attempt to drive the images of food from her brain, she heard another noise from outside the garage. This noise was from a roughly running vehicle of some type, probably a pickup truck with a muffler, which was either seriously damaged, or ripped off. As she listened intently, she heard the sounds of goods being piled roughly into a vehicle. Next, she heard several vehicle doors slam, followed by the vehicle pulling away from her hiding spot.

Samantha wasn't sure whether to wait for a while or to venture out of the garage. She could tell that the sun was approaching the horizon, given how the light was getting as it leaked into the garage from around the edge of the door. She tried convincing herself to wait until darkness was complete, but she found that the pangs of hunger from her stomach wouldn't permit her to wait. As quietly as she could, she lowered the ladder from the attic and positioned it carefully. Next, she climbed down the ladder and crept over to the door of the garage.

As she had expected, the door wasn't locked, only latched. Slowly, she eased the door open and looked out into the yard. Seeing nothing out of the ordinary, she crept out of the garage and edged along the wall until she could look around to the front of the building. Again, having seen nothing out of the ordinary, she retraced the path she had taken to the garage the night before and discovered her makeshift pike still laying in the dry grass. Quickly, she retrieved the pike and then began to cut through the backyards, away from the despised garage.

Unsure of exactly where she was going, she continued to dart between houses while always keeping the setting sun to her right. This, she knew, meant that she was heading south, which was the shortest direction out of the town. But she also knew that she wouldn't be able to keep moving for more than a few more minutes, until darkness had enveloped her. And with the growing pangs of hunger in her stomach, she would need to find something to eat soon, or her strength, which was already marginal, would begin to fade even more.

.

ABOUT THE ANGRY EAGLE ANTHOLOGIES

Angry Eagle Publishing, LLC offers anthologies in all genres. Opening up new opportunities for new writers and an outlet for those who've been at it a while to try out new genres. Knows for it's mentoring and ability to showcase new writers the Angry Eagle Anthology Project has seen a number of success stories.

Our Anthologies

Apocalyptic Winter [Book one]
Anarchy
Apocalyptic Winter [Book Two]

Coming in 2020

Anthologies in:
Horror
Fantasy
Zompoc
Sci-fi

Hop on board and send us a story.
http://www.angryeaglepublishing.com/home/anthology-submission/

Made in the USA
Coppell, TX
15 March 2026

73912744R00118